radio belly

stories
RADIO

BELLY
buffy cram

Douglas & McIntyre
D&M PUBLISHERS INC.
Vancouver/Toronto/Berkeley

Douglas & McIntyre
An imprint of D&M Publishers Inc.
2323 Quebec Street, Suite 201
Vancouver BC Canada V5T 4S7
www.douglas-mcintyre.com

Cataloguing data available from Library and Archives Canada
ISBN 978-1-55365-902-0 (pbk.) · ISBN 978-1-55365-903-7 (ebook)

Editing by Barbara Berson
Cover and text design by Peter Cocking
Cover illustration by Brian Tong
Printed and bound in Canada by Friesens
Distributed in the U.S. by Publishers Group West

We gratefully acknowledge the financial support of the Canada Council for the Arts, the British Columbia Arts Council, the Province of British Columbia through the Book Publishing Tax Credit and the Government of Canada through the Canada Book Fund for our publishing activities.

For my mom:
my best friend and number one fan.

contents

mineral by
mineral

IF IT WERE POSSIBLE to pinpoint a beginning, it would have to be *Punctuation Camp!*, a publicity stunt the boss arranged to promote a new educational series.

Instead of cleaning out filing cabinets or pretending to look busy—all the things that usually fill an ordinary week—everyone from the Children's Division of Crawford & Hicks Publishing is forced to dress up like various punctuation marks, in all the colours of the rainbow: a period, a comma, a hyphen, a colon and semicolon. Even quotation marks, as conjoined twins: the "66 Sisters" and "99 Brothers." Out of the deep sleep of autumn, everyone must conjure good cheer, climb aboard the "Punctuation Bus!" and spend the week driving from one school to another.

This is how, in her thirtieth year, immediately following a breakup and a demotion from the department of real, adult literature—in what the boss is now calling "the shuffle"—Shana ends up dressed as an exclamation point. As if she were Gumby's uptight relative, her body is encased in a block of green foam from her knees to well above her head. Only her face, arms and black-spandex calves poke out of the costume. Her feet, surrounded by foam, are the "point" of her exclamation.

On the first morning of camp, Shana and the other punctuation marks shuffle around a gymnasium while teachers give lessons to groups of "attention- or otherwise-challenged" kids. It's explained that these kids are "very inner-city." Shana's instructed not to make prolonged eye contact, not to linger, to move quickly and speak only in exclamatory statements: "Punctuation is fun!" and "Clap your hands!" and "Good job, kids!"

Lunch has its own set of challenges. In no mood for portion control, Shana eats fast and hard, getting mayo all over her costume, tomato seeds in her hair. Then one of the 99 Brothers leans in mid-sandwich and teases, "Don't forget to breathe," loud enough for the whole room to hear, so Shana ends up having to tell her new co-workers the same thing she told her old co-workers: that she has a rare illness, the only cure being a "special, high-calorie diet." If she didn't eat this way, her body would waste away, she says.

In the afternoon, the "Punctuation Team!" attempts to act out skits while the students burn off whatever they've had for lunch and/or show what they've learned. It quickly becomes evident that they have retained nothing though. The kids rally around, beating the foam shells of the costumes with sticky hands, hugging, kicking and grabbing various parts of anatomy. This is when Shana first interacts with Phoebe, the young Ivy League intern she'll be sharing an office with the following week, and the only person with a costume more cumbersome than her own—whenever Phoebe turns too quickly, and no matter how much frenzied back-pedalling she does, the immense curve of her question mark brings her down. But Phoebe's cheer is relentless. As soon as she's back on her feet she's playing the befuddled question mark again. Pulling Phoebe back up for the second time, Shana starts to get pissed off on her behalf. She begins to feel detached, even monstrous. She wants to level with these kids: "It's time to let your learning limitations guide you! Most of you will become mechanics, carpenters, waitresses, escorts—and punctuation won't even matter!" She wants to instill fear, to hurl their lisping, soft bodies at the walls.

While helping each other out of their costumes at the end of the day, Shana discovers Phoebe is one of those vegetarian, volunteering, virgin-till-married types. Still, she can't help admiring Phoebe's ability to stay in character even after the show's over. If Shana's sentences are dragged down by the lead weight of negativity, then Phoebe's are helium balloons, light as air, despite her costume's structural challenges. They'll never be friends, that's clear, but for some reason Shana still confides in Phoebe about the three-car-pile-up of her life: entering a new decade, being dumped and getting demoted all within a few weeks of each other.

THE NEXT MONDAY, when Shana has finally managed to put *Punctuation Camp!* behind her, she's called into the boss's office and reprimanded for saying "Fuck!" in front of the children too often, for having chased a group of them to the back of the gym yelling, "Avoid the wrath of words!"

"They don't even know what 'wrath' means," Shana argues. "It was a game! Like tag."

But her boss isn't convinced. "Need I remind you about the girl with the pigtails?" she asks.

The girl with rubber boots and a mustard-stained mouth had come stomping after Shana, sour-faced, fists flailing as soon as they'd made eye contact and yet, everyone seems to agree it's *Shana* who has done something wrong. Apparently it isn't okay for punctuation to restrain a child by the pigtails under any circumstances, ever. Apparently Shana was sufficiently warned about the dangers of eye contact.

"And the eating?" Shana's boss asks next.

"Oh, that?" Shana says. "I have this thing. It's like hypoglycemia, except it's hypo-something else."

As a kid she used to sit at the table stuffing as many grapes/blueberries/cherries into her mouth as she could. She'd bite down, eyes and cheeks bursting, juice running down her chin to her neck. This was the only way to really taste food, she was sure. As she grew older, the hunger grew. These days it's a whole watermelon, a box of doughnuts, an entire Deep 'n Delicious cake in one sitting.

Shana manages to smooth things over with the boss by agreeing to "see someone." As for Phoebe, after just a few days in the office together it's clear she'll never evolve beyond her punctuation role. Everything she says is delivered the same way—with a perky flip to her words, somewhere between questioning and stupidity. And that wide-eyed, overenthusiastic expression she used to captivate a room full of ADD kids: it turns out that's her actual personality.

IN THE WEEKS after *Punctuation Camp!*, the person Shana has agreed to see—Wendy is her name—encourages Shana to "acknowledge her anger." It's true, Shana admits, digging her finger into the small planter on the coffee table in Wendy's office—she *is* mad. At everything. Always.

She regularly shows open malice toward those tourists who twirl in the middle of the sidewalk, pointing this way and that like bloated weather vanes, oblivious to the commuter surge around them. At coffee shops she orders non-fat, ristretto lattes, then accuses the barista of not knowing what *ristretto* means, sounding the word out, "Ri-*stret*-to," her voice in the distinct octave of anger. Everywhere she goes she tests the limits of customer service. Once passive-aggressive, she's now just aggressive.

She's also mad at the businessmen, hunched like little boys at the too-small tables of these coffee shops. Mad at the way they peer over the rims of their paper cups, not just at her but *into* her, as if invited to lounge, belly-up on the (white leather) couch of her innermost soul. These are the men no one else wants—desperate men with eyes like open caves, eyes that give her the feeling she's being pulled into a fishy darkness against her will. She wants to tell them, "This attraction is *all* you, *all* imagined," but she doesn't have time for eyes. What's worse are the men who don't look. The ones who go as far as shoes-knees-waist, then back to their papers/phones/americanos. Assholes. When she was younger, men's eyes at least made the traverse to arrive at her face. Now it's like her midriff is a mountain range, a jungle on fire—impassable.

She's mad that the only thing she can listen to since David left is punk—songs like "Fuck the World" and "A Good Day to Kill"—because it approximates the noise in her head. Mad that musicians insist on padding CDs these days with verbal interludes, that every open space left in the city is just like one of those interludes: maximized, crammed with a neon sign, a billboard. It seems the world is full of words and noise—all of it embedding itself into her brain like shrapnel.

But that's not all she's mad at.

She's mad that elementary school seems to have been the best time of her life, that the lid on her favourite travel mug has a leak in it (again), that she just bought the entire bedroom set from pages 84–85 of the IKEA catalogue, yet morning still feels like a punch to the gut.

And she's mad at her desk-to-chair-height ratio at work, at the resulting case of what her chiropractor calls "mouse arm." Mad that what pains her most in this world has been given a name like "mouse arm," robbing her of all due sympathy.

Wendy gets Shana to admit all of this, and then she puts her pencil to her lips and says, sweet as can be, "Now, what can you tell me about hunger?"

Shana doesn't mean to ignore the question. It's just that she's still focused on the plant on the table before her. It's that wispy kind of fern that requires daily watering. The soil is darker than most, grainy, probably freshly fertilized with that organic stuff full of trace minerals.

Shana's friends recommend medication, meditation, chakra cleansing, ear coning and rereading her favourite novels to figure out how and why her life has come to this. "Fuck off," she says invariably, before changing the subject. She almost says the same when Wendy first mentions taking pottery classes, but something—call it self-control—gets in the way. Or maybe it's the way Wendy watches Shana, with her pencil and notepad at the ready. It makes Shana think this pottery thing is more than a mere suggestion. Her job may depend upon it.

The classes are held in the basement of a community college in a long, cold room reminiscent of a public change room or a morgue: damp, echoey, with a certain underwater quality to the light. Shana sits across from a woman named Grace who wears a hand-knit sweater and galoshes. Grace has let her grey roots grow out to the halfway point and Shana can't help but admire her for this. Everyone is given a slab of clay and told to knead and pound it against the table. For the first half of class Shana keeps up, copying the teacher's movements, but eventually she ends up sitting and watching as Grace dips her hands in water and runs her wet fingers across the clay, turning it, smoothing it, over and over. It's all that grey water, the smell of it, that causes a thread of drool to yo-yo out Shana's mouth and puddle on the table. Grace looks up at Shana, then down at the drool, but her hands never break pace.

SHANA TAKES HERSELF out for hamburgers and modifies the order to include extra fries, extra bacon, extra burger. On the drive home she stops to buy bags of beef jerky, salmon jerky, turkey jerky. Then, to forgive herself, to forget, she eats whole boxes of mandarin oranges in the dark of her bedroom, fast and all at once.

"YOU HAVEN'T BEEN eating well," Shana's mom says and then promptly signs her up for mail-order supplements.

"You need to appreciate what you *do* have," says Phoebe. This from the girl who is visiting Shana's life on an internship, a one-semester layover on the way to something better.

"You're not the same," Shana's friends say. They've been eyeing her closely since David left for law school on the warmer coast.

It's true. Nothing's the same. Not since that last good-bye in his bright and empty kitchen, the smell of aftershave and espresso on his skin. Not since he asked, "Sure you can't come?" with all the intonation of "Want a drink?" Such a bounding, reckless question. Such casual delivery.

Her friends and her mom and Phoebe are right. She hasn't been herself. Not since David's phone calls thinned and then stopped. Not since her final, desperate call and his confession: "Yes, there's someone. You'd like her. Reminds me of you." Someone he knew as a kid, someone he'd eaten Play-Doh with more than three decades ago. Perhaps the only someone who could make her and David's last year and a quarter together seem like one of those noisy interludes, an intermission in some other, greater story. This girl (his fiancée, he'd finally admitted) has eclipsed Shana entirely. "Thanks for teaching me to love. You were right, I wasn't open," David said before Shana hung up on him.

Maybe *that's* where all the anger comes from.

But maybe that's not it at all. David was good in a three-times-per-week kind of way. Sure, they were sexually compatible—predictable for a couple of pent-up office workers. They could share a holiday, a tropical vacation—but a lifetime? Maybe this has nothing to do with David. The world is angry, after all. Fires, floods and quakes. It's trying to shake us off, Shana thinks. Perhaps she's a geyser steaming on account of something greater, something subterranean. Or maybe she just hoped her life would be different by now. By this age she'd expected love. Celebrity. Wealth. Satiety. But instead this: an ordinary road and she an empty bucket rolling down it, the hollow thud waking people in the night. Instead, anger, hunger.

SOME OTHER THINGS Wendy leads Shana to admit:

She's a bit of a snob. She runs her social life like big business or corporate America, with mergers and trades. Only her prettiest friends make the cut. She and these friends dress up, meet over (artisanal, fair trade) coffees or (herbal-infused) martinis and proceed to psychoanalyze the moves and missteps of acquaintances like a bunch of retired players scrutinizing the game at halftime.

Sometimes she lies. On a bad day, the lies come one after another, awkward and tumbling. Simple lies: "Yes, I've kissed a girl. No, I don't watch TV. Yes, I'm fluent in Spanish."

No going back then. She blinks, lets the words clang in her ears, smiles. Her world shrinks ever so slightly. These are the people she must avoid from now on, the ones she's lied to for no good reason.

If she had a warning label, it would read: "Good friend, not great. Talks more than listens. May or may not have a conscience. Manipulative in an emergency. Needs constant attention. May or may not be capable of authentic connections. Should not be exposed to displays of sickness, grief, shame. May contain traces of fraudulence."

AT THE SECOND pottery class Shana discovers that if she hangs around long enough afterwards, she's free to wander among all the fresh-cut clay. Down in that underwater room, where sound bounces off the walls, it's easy to forget the lies, the friends, work. Everything retreats, as in the moments before sleep. She lifts the damp cloths covering the slabs of clay and admires their dense edges, her mouth watering, breath shallow, legs quivering as she breaks a piece off and rubs the creamy, rich mud between her fingers. This is a slippery secretion, she thinks, something straight from the world's wet, hot mouth. She imagines earth moving through her, coating her insides with mineral slime and, just to know what it feels like, she brings a smear of clay to her lips.

Rubbing that clay over tongue and teeth, it's easy to recall that there has always been a hunger. One bite and some part of her rushes way out ahead, while another, wiser part stays behind. It's a downhill, speedy feeling, like the body falling away. It's a Tarzan moment, her willpower caught in the middle of a jungle swoop. Something quiet speaks to her: *More.* She obeys. Chews. Swallows. Then the voice returns, stronger: *MoreMoreMore.*

In the following weeks, it isn't just clay she craves. Soil too. At the dinner parties of so-called friends, Shana finds herself fishing it out of terra cotta pots by the handful. She disappears into second-storey bathrooms to choke it back, gagging as if on mouthfuls of sawdust until she learns to add water, to swirl it in her mouth, to let it glide down. This, she decides, is the final "fuck you," spitting chunks of fertilizer like chicken bones into the designer sinks of the newly married, those very friends who claim Shana is the one that changed.

THE END COMES on a Friday a few weeks later. Shana arrives at the office late, having just fought her way through the ass-end of a hurricane.

"How *aaare* you, sweetie?" Phoebe asks in an impossible pitch, her eyebrows turned up in cartoon-faced concern.

"Shitty," Shana answers. She's all gloom and baritone, in an effort to bring Phoebe down a notch. Then she realizes how tired she is of this role, how sick she is of Phoebe wearing her emotions all over her face, asking obvious questions before she's even in the door, calling her *sweetie,* of all things. Salty, Saucy, Skanky—fine—but not *sweetie.*

"I was stuck behind some stupid cunt all the way up Boylston," Shana continues.

Phoebe's face scrunches up. "What did you just say?"

"Boylston," Shana replies.

Phoebe doesn't react, seems to be frozen on the spot, so Shana goes about her business, turning on the computer, checking voice mail.

"No," she finally says, stepping out from behind her desk. "You said the C-word." It may be the first time Phoebe's made an actual statement, the first authentic expression Shana's seen on her pretty little face, but now it's Shana's turn to withhold reaction. She fiddles with her e-mail. Touché.

Phoebe leans across Shana's desk, suddenly emboldened, like this is a showdown, Shana's desk a saloon bar. "The C-word," she says.

Shana lets her lean closer, closer still, then yells at close range, "She was a *cunt!*"

She pretends not to notice Phoebe's frozen-faced disgust, as if the whole world spins on this one four-letter word. As if Shana has dropped a cunt-bomb onto her tender little mind and things will never be the same.

In the silence that follows, and feeling a certain charge in the air, Shana starts to wonder if things ever will be the same. She's discovered a word with some actual power, and Phoebe is so rattled that she's decided to take an early coffee break. *Good riddance. Cunt.* But before long the boss angles in the doorway and asks Shana to come to her office. Her features are taut, stapled down, her lipstick fierce.

Sitting back in the houndstooth chair in her corner office, the boss explains that Phoebe has been keeping track of Shana's profanities, that the C-word is crossing a line, and Shana should take a few days to "cool down" and "reprioritize." Words reach Shana as if from a great distance. She nods, thinking only of the potted plant in her office—a corn plant, freshly watered, with wide, dark leaves.

Once the boss sets her free, Shana rushes back to her own office, goes straight to that corn plant, dips both hands in the cool, silky soil and brings it to her mouth, handful after handful. *I am animal,* she thinks, fingernails caked with dirt and drool, *all action and reaction.* Then, Phoebe's desk. She walks over and begins riffling through papers, her weekly planner, files and drawers, leaving muddy prints the whole way.

"MINERAL DEFICIENCY," Shana's doctor says, practically watering at the mouth, delighted that Shana's body has at last produced something more compelling than a yeast infection. "But we should do rigorous testing," she continues, spitting out the words, "to rule out something more serious." She sputters on about the possibility of a brain tumour or impending stroke, about the procedure for proving there *is* a medical basis to Shana's recent outbursts. She keeps talking about the "incidents" at work, the need to get Shana's life "back on track." Wet words. Shana wants to ask about the medical implications of loneliness or wrong turns. Instead—because she's sorry she even came here, because she's on some kind of roll—she calls the doctor an oversimplistic bitch and leaves.

Out on the sidewalk, squinting and stumbling in the bright white sun, Shana recalls having once heard that anger is just self-hatred that misses its mark. And something uplifting too, about one door closing so that another can open.

She has always been hungry, it's true. It's the same hunger now, just a more mature version. So many kinds of earth: red, black, brown. Silt. Clay. It's earth she's been after all along. The source of all things. The quickest route to her cravings. It's earth that tastes like everything her body has ever wanted. Like flesh or blood but cleaner. Like raw potatoes or fish skin. The musty updraft after rain. The beginnings of the world.

She recalls reading about an elderly woman who went out for milk one December day, slipped and fell headfirst into a ten-foot mound of snow on a busy corner. This was no clean drift either, but one of those piss-yellow piles left by the city plows, a gravelly mound with an air pocket. No family to notice her absence. Traffic spraying past. She wasn't found until the thaw. It is this thought, of an old woman's sensible pumps and bruised ankles sticking out of the snow, the thought that the city itself might be hungry, that sends Shana home and makes her stay.

All she wants is to sit on the floor in the middle of her apartment—TV off, radio off, lights off—and want nothing. She imagines she is an island (here fending off visions of mangoes/pineapples/drinks with umbrellas) caught up in something huge and ancient. Continental drift. The slow-change of landforms. She wants to give herself over to a geological sense of time. To fathom the passage of ice ages. Generations. To cast herself back to a time when four-letter words and casual answers to casual questions didn't threaten existence, a time of preliteracy.

She imagines roots (but not tubers, not potato chips or French fries) spreading like needy hands, cracking concrete above, displacing soil below. She thinks of ore being blasted, crushed down to unearth something that glints: gold, agate, quartz, running in seams, great underground ribbons (not layers of fudge or buckets of ice cream. Not spoons in pursuit of chocolate-covered almonds. Not caramel. Not marshmallows). She is not allowed to think of food. This is the number one rule. She is allowed to drink water if she wants. It helps her feel geological. She is allowed to think of minerals and the generations of men who have lusted after them, their dry hands and mouths, their bones now turned to dust.

IT IS ON a day like this. It is after hours of lying spread-eagled on the floor, forcing her breath from deep to shallow until she is just skimming the surface, just barely touching down with water-spider legs on the surface of what it means to be alive. It is after days of drinking only water, of imagining a body in decay, of trying to picture the exact moment when it becomes more earth than flesh that she realizes she is relieved her boyfriend is gone (and her job and her friends). That her mineral cravings are stronger than any feelings she had for those things. That what she really wants is to be alone, to fall away and be absorbed, mineral by mineral. Not to eat the dirt, but to have the dirt eat her. She breathes, deep this time, and the surface ripples.

On the other hand, Shana thinks, maybe all this dirt-eating and swearing is just another kind of life reaching out to her. Not a breaking down but a breaking through. Perhaps there is a life far from this city with its man-eating slush piles. She imagines a wide-open sky and a life lived under it.

She thinks of the type of people who watch that sky—day in, day out—as if it were the world news, all there is to know.

Perhaps she'll get in her (red hatchback) Honda and drive for days without stopping, turning at last into some desperate, landlocked town to find an honest husband who comes home hungry from a long day bent over his good work. Perhaps she will have children, three, and a garden she will talk about as if it were her fourth. Perhaps a house with drafty floors and windowsills that weep, a wood stove and gumboots by the back door. And perhaps she will love those children and that husband and that garden in a way that makes her forget herself. Perhaps she's not so different from her mother and her mother's mother after all. Maybe from now on she will allow herself the pleasures she never thought were good enough.

Or, her Honda might follow the birds south this winter, south until the water swirls the other way and everything—the fruit, the language, the constellations—is made new again. Perhaps she'll raise llamas and live in a house shaped like a teardrop in the very centre of a desert. Maybe watching the sand dunes shift and the sky rearrange itself and her animals swell and burst year after year, reaching into their groaning bodies to pull out their young—the blood, the sweat, the matted fur—will deliver something of the miracle of life to her.

Perhaps she'll come off birth control and stop showering all together.

Or perhaps, soon, she will swallow her last mouthful of dirt, lick her teeth clean, and know: That is all, enough.

Nothing broken—down or through. Perhaps then she'll know with certainty that she'd only ever meant to go up to this edge, not over, that like a cartographer of inner space, it was the view she was after, that she had merely wanted to know her way to this edge and to know her way back.

loveseat

WHEN I FIRST saw her, she was alone in the corner at a house party. She was all painted up—purple lips, hair a bluish-black and a tropical glow to her skin. I noticed she was putting back a glass of wine and a fistful of peanuts, not even tasting them so much as trying to throw them right at the problem. The problem, as far as I could see it? A rabbit hole where her heart should be, something gaping and vulnerable and with its own gravitational field—everything inwards, everything down. I saw this right away and you have to understand, Jason Jenson has never been much for seeing things. But the strangest part was I wanted to give myself over to that problem right away, to be swallowed whole with the rest of the peanuts.

She wasn't exactly small, even then, and I'm not one to talk about auras, but I could see something shimmering around her. The potential for all that flesh—what it wanted to be. Skin like toasted pastry. Big breasts pushed up and together until they made a straight line down her chest. When I finally got close, I could hear her body calling out to me. *Hot cross buns,* her sibilant breasts were saying, *Eat us! Love us!*

I guess she saw me staring because she stuck out a puffy hand and said her name was Laureen. So what'd I do? I told her that was the worst name I'd ever heard, that it sounded like the last noise before a car wreck. Then I said something starting with, "Is that your face or..." and laughed at my own joke—*haw-haw-haw*—like I was doing the morning show. Thing is, in those days I was all morning show, all the time. I was really somebody and I needed everyone to know it.

I waited for her comeback, but instead she gave a hurt little smile, a crumpled croissant, and I could see I'd lost a fan.

"Sorry," I said. "You ever suddenly realize what a dick you are?"

"No," she said, "but I realize what a dick *you* are."

I choked on air, squirmed a bit.

"One more chance," she said, and that was that. Bingo-bango, I was hooked. People say it takes months to fall in love. Not true. With me and Laureen it took all of two minutes. The rest was just fallout.

"NO *WAY!* You're Jenson the *Jet?*" Laureen said later that night, licking salt and peanut skin from her long nails, the kind with the white stripe across the top. "I wake up at 8:25 every morning. Sometimes you're the only reason I get out of bed."

The five-minute spot that had made me famous: 8:25 to 8:30. "Get the Jet" was the name of the segment. This was in the days before Google so the rules were simple: five minutes of rock 'n' roll trivia from random callers; for each question I got right, we added money to the prize pot; the first person to "Get the Jet" got the money. Innocent enough, except I'd been undefeated for two years running and in that time the jackpot had climbed to over $20,000. I can't explain what happened next. Maybe all that money brought out the mean in people, or maybe, this being a time before road rage, the commuters just needed an outlet. Either way, at some point the people banded together and started hurling trash talk along with their questions. Naturally, I hurled it back. It was a strange time in radio—that era between Casey Kasem and Howard Stern—and this was something brand new. Ratings jumped and the sponsors came running.

It must've looked like the Jet was flying pretty high, but the truth is in the months just before meeting Laureen, the bottom had fallen out of the whole thing. The talk had become more vicious, the questions harder, and I had no connection to the music anymore. Every guy with a guitar, every four-man band, it all sounded like the same damn song to me—all lonely howl and hammering need, just like every day of our long, sorry lives, the same parts reassembled. Alarm-clock ring and bleary-eyed commute. Drive-through coffee and donuts. Tired old jokes sandwiched between commercials and news. The same days and weeks and years circling back on us. I was tired of the insults, tired of the trick questions. All I wanted was a little human kindness.

Now, any DJ hoping to keep a career at a classic rock station knows to keep their Grateful Dead inclinations under wraps because, as far as the station manager's concerned, there are classic rock fans and there are Deadheads; a person can't be both. A good radio boss knows that if you're in "the family" it's just a matter of time before you start waxing live about the time Jerry played "Looks Like Rain" in Indiana and, lo and behold, a minute into the jam, the sky opened up and what'd it do? It rained. Oh boy, did it rain. You've never been so wet in your life.

I never believed it would happen to me, but when things got rough, it was the family I turned to.

I started playing bootlegs: old live cuts of rehearsals, all stops and restarts, the notes so loose they barely hung together; scratchy recordings where the front-stage banter was as loud as the music—"China Cat Sunflower" interrupted by "Hey, man, quit crowdin' my girl."

I even had Deadheads calling up with their concert "miracles" and I told my own: the time I was walking along the highway outside a Michigan concert, one finger held up to the sky the way every Deadhead needing a ticket did in those days, finger like a lightning rod trying to bring down a miracle, the thunderclouds rolling in on the horizon. Just when I started to think I'd missed another one, some guy with a military cut and khakis pulled up in a station wagon beside me and handed over a stack of tickets saying, "My son won't be needin' these," then got back in his car and drove off.

The new Grateful Dead content had cured me, I'd tapped into the fount of human kindness, but the morning show producers weren't pleased. The very same day I met Laureen, I was called into their office. "No more of this touchy-feely miracle shit," they said. "Put on some Steppenwolf and get back to the trash talk. That's an order."

"I REALLY GET what you're doing lately," Laureen said that first night, leaning forward. She smelled just like a piña colada. "I'm a huge fan."

"Thanks," I said, and for the first time in a long time I meant it.

"No, of The Dead," she said. "I mean, I like you too, but I'm a huge fan of The Dead." She must've said some other stuff then about growing up on the road, but I wasn't paying attention.

I was watching her dark purple mouth, thinking it was shaped just like a heart. Thinking, who could resist a girl who walks around with her heart on her face like that? She turned to the TV, poured another glass of wine, threw it back, chewed her thumb, spat a piece of skin.

And that's when it started. Both of us saying the same thing at the same time, filling our first awkward silence in exactly the same way:

Her and me: "You're different."

Me and her: "What?"

Us: "Stop that."

No longer two: "What the hell?"

One: "Get out of my head."

Me: "I mean, you're more forgiving than most listeners."

Her: "I mean, you're more human, flawed."

We stared at each other. We were two voices again, two heads, four eyes, ten senses—possibly twelve—stinging from the wet slap of separation, the air between us moist and electric. And that's it, the last moment before Jenson the Jet went the way of the peanuts, down Laureen's black hole with his best intentions, his ego, his sense of identity. Down he went and did he mind?

THERE WAS A brief interval here in which we attempted to get to know each other the usual way. There were late-night phone calls. I asked about her family. She said it was complicated. I asked about her work. She said she was at the cutting edge of sunless tanning—cream not bulbs. I asked her on a date, which led to an inevitable first kiss. It started on my front stoop on a Friday night, lips pressed sweetly, the two of us fumbling through the door, tripping over shoes all the way down the hall, soft slurping through the rest of the apartment and into the bedroom where, for three tongue-smashing days, we created our own language of licks and murmurs. At some point she slept and I adored her long enough to see her fingernails grow.

We emerged on Monday night famished, dehydrated and weakened by the miracles we'd encountered: of the human body, and of the love two people can go without for so long, of being two but being one and, finally, of having become so enamoured and so raw, as though over the course of three days we'd unpeeled each other and were now soft grapes bumping up against all the hard things of this world.

We never did get around to the long walks or commitment conversations because when she finally went to leave the bed on that Monday night, her wide, pale back (the only part of her body she couldn't reach with her tanning creams) curled and hunched up-down, up-down. She was crying, and it was right up there with the saddest things I'd ever seen, along with stillborn puppies and, once at a museum in the South, a pink baby floating in a green-glass bottle. Then she turned to me and said, "I don't think I can ever go back to my life," and the thing is, I didn't think I could either.

TURNS OUT THE producers were wrong. The family was alive and well and everywhere. Ratings spiked. The morning show was getting listeners from all walks of life now: lawyers, teachers, housewives, runaways. Not only that, the family had people in high places. We were getting syndication offers, advertising dollars, airlines phoning up to add to the prize pot just because I had the word *Jet* in my name.

I married Laureen, got us a nice three-room apartment at the top of a glass tower and told the producers I'd be taking calls from home now. Those were the days. A little bit of trivia every morning and the rest of the time I helped Laureen pursue her passion. Fantasy Tan, Tahitian Breeze, Vanilla Beach, Caribbean Dream: she became a distributor of the latest and greatest self-tanning products. She ordered vats of lotions, transferred them into smaller bottles and dispatched them to salons all over the city. While I read up on rock 'n' roll history, she kept track of clients and products, imports and exports.

We gave our own skin over for testing. Laureen had calves in mind, but I wanted to transform the sad, blank canvas of her back. She monitored the product closely in the mirror for ease of application, grease or streak factor, its sheerness, its sheen, its fadeability. *"Fadeability* isn't a word," I told her, but she didn't care.

We had six months of relative happiness. Six brief and beautiful months before I noticed just how much of a fan Laureen was. When she wasn't in her office talking tan, she was in the living room with me, talking Jerry. It was Jerry-this and Jerry-that. It was, "Most people don't know this..." and "Did you ever hear about the time..." almost as if she thought she knew more than me. Then came the questions: "What instruments did he play before the guitar?" and "How much did he weigh at his heaviest?" and "Where did his mother's mother grow up?" I'll admit there were times when I wondered if she really did know more than me, times when I wondered if I'd married my nemesis, the one person who could bring me down. I wondered if life could be so cruel. Then I just decided to put my foot down: no more Jerry-talk in the house. It was messing with my trivia, I said, not to mention our marriage.

She started taking her work very seriously after that. She started using the creams in excess—skimming off the top like any good dealer—and turned a deep orange, like carrots gone bad. She started wearing sundresses in the middle of winter, sunglasses in the house. I tried to steer her toward jeans and sweaters. I tried to love her for better or for worse, but I hardly recognized her anymore and that coconut smell was everywhere. She was making phone calls to women named Candy, Cindy, Carmen and Christy at all hours of the night: "You're really gonna like this one, hon. Glides on smooth and acts fast. What they're calling an *island tan*," I'd hear her say through the walls. It was during one of these calls I overheard her say she grew up in "the family." I couldn't believe what I was hearing—*the* family, not *a* family. This was a direct threat to my career, my identity, everything I held dear. I barged in on her. "You never told me you grew up in the *family*-family," I screamed. She claimed she'd told me that first night. I said maybe I would've heard her if she hadn't been garburating peanuts in my ear the whole time. Her chin wobbled and I realized the Jet had gone too far. I apologized and offered to rub her favourite tanning cream onto her back. It took a whole week of backrubs. My palms had turned a ruddy orange by the time I was done, but I eventually got the whole story out of her.

After the Grateful Dead came out of their one-year hiatus in '75, when so many people were convinced the band's days were numbered, Laureen's mom and a bunch of college friends pooled their money and bought a decommissioned school bus. It was beet-red and rusted so badly they could see highway passing through holes in the floor, but it ran well. They took out the benches, covered the holes with plywood, put in hot plates, beds, hammocks, curtains, and every year, May to August, they hit the road. All through their childhoods, Laureen and a handful of other kids spent their summers chasing the Grateful Dead across America, concert to concert, camping at lakes and rivers in between.

At concerts, the moms would go with the girls from the bus to the mud pit in front of the stage, where they'd spin in their sundresses for hours: wild-haired, sandals stomping, daisy chains flying. Laureen knew all the words to all the songs, and she swears that sometimes she knew, *just knew,* which song was coming up next. She was so good that, in those loose moments between songs when the band pulled close to Jerry, people in the pit pulled close to Laureen—kids, moms and strangers, too—asking what was next, and let's just say Laureen was right more often than she was wrong.

"I don't know what the big deal was," Laureen explained. "I spent half my childhood looking up Jerry's nose. You'd think I'd know the guy."

But she didn't have me fooled. The Dead were the greatest jam band in history. Nobody knew what they were going to play next; that was the whole point.

ON THE MORNING of August 9, 1995, I woke up to the sound of whimpering. It was early, still dark. I found her leaning over the kitchen sink, where the knife was lying in a mess of blood and dishes. It was the middle finger on her right hand, cut to the bone. She had been loading the sink, she said, and hadn't even known she was hurt until she saw the blood.

In my hasty search for a towel, I remember glancing at the oven clock: 4:23 a.m. By the time I had her hand wrapped, it had already happened: "Jerry's dead," she said, and she was so shaken, so small, I didn't even think to ask how she knew.

She refused to go to the hospital, so I bandaged her up and put her to bed. I told her a story: of two minds joining over a bowl of peanuts, of a woman who paints all the women of the world a truer colour. "They're all starlets now, baby," I whispered, "Tahitian starlets," but she was inconsolable.

She kept muttering that she had done this, turned her back on him, and some other things too, about devouring the things she loves, about people's eggshell edges and sucking the yolk out through the cracks.

It didn't reach the news until much later that morning: Jerry Garcia, dead of a heart attack at exactly 4:23 a.m. Out of respect, I cancelled the trivia segment. I used the extra time to do some research. I found out he played the piano before the guitar, that at his heaviest he weighed over three hundred pounds, that indeed it was the middle finger of his right hand he'd accidentally severed while chopping wood as a kid—but all the while I was wondering, what kind of a person wakes up to do dishes at four in the morning?

LAUREEN STOPPED LEAVING the house, stopped running the business, stopped dressing. She kept me busy though. There were things she needed from the outside world: nail polish and hair dye, waxes and creams, smoothers and straighteners. She wanted loofahs and exfoliants, tweezers and extractors, shavers and strange glues. She wanted food, too: biryani and bulgogi, bibimbap and tabbouleh, donburi and dal, vindaloo, kulcha, edamame and udon. Every day she grew more demanding. She wanted something more exotic, harder to find. She wanted it hotter or colder or saltier or faster. And more, she always wanted more. When she wasn't eating, she was in the bathroom, primping and painting herself. She never failed to tune into my show though. I'd hear a small tinny version of myself playing on the other side of the door. I'd hear her cackling, talking back to the radio, heckling me or heckling them—it was hard to tell which. For months I was at her beck and call. I brought her what she asked for and never once complained. Anything to keep her happy.

Sequestered in the world of our apartment, she started to grow: first two hundred pounds, then on her way to three. And while she grew, in equal and direct proportions, I shrank. The day I found the letters, I was down to a hundred pounds, a mere whiff of a man. I'd started to look vacuum-packed, the bones of my face lunging forward while my cheeks and eye sockets sunk inwards.

I found three shoeboxes full of letters. *My Dear Laureen, My Heart, My Darling Lo-Lo* they read, every last one of them signed by Jerry. I had to sit when I found them. It was the weight of the boxes against my jutting-out bones and it was something else, too—a memory from my first concert. I hadn't found tickets in time, so I'd spent the night of the show camped on a garbage-strewn beach at the edge of the concert grounds. I fell asleep feeling sorry for myself. No ticket, no tent, no blanket, no miracles, and all my favourite songs distorted by the distance. Then, the next morning I woke up at an hour when the sky and water were the exact same shade of blue, and in that stillness I got my "miracle" after all—not the ticket kind but that other kind you sometimes hear about. I watched an eagle circle and then dive in front of me—as menacing as it was graceful. It rose up triumphant, with a huge fish in its claws, but that fish wouldn't quit. It twisted and fought in the air, bringing them both lower and lower until eventually they were thrashing on the surface of the water. They struggled for some time, the eagle beating its wings until its feathers were wet, heavy, the fish muscling its tail into the air.

Sitting there on the floor, with the box of letters in my lap, I remembered there was a quiet moment, when the eagle stood still on the back of the fish, tilted half in, half out of the water. Then, finally, with a sudden twist of its tail the fish pulled the big, majestic bird under and the water was still again. The thing was, with the lake and sky the exact same colour, they probably both thought they were winning.

THERE WERE TEN years of letters, about one a week from the last decade of Jerry's life. He talked about two minds joining in the darkness and all the ways two people can feel like one, even across time and space. He talked about back-stage and under-stage and side-stage encounters.

I asked if there was anything she'd forgotten to tell me, if she had secrets, unfinished business with anyone. No, none, nothing, she said. I started pouring salt onto her food, melted butter. I was loading her up with saturated fat, MSG, ingredients I couldn't pronounce the names of. I stopped going out for hair dye, contacts, nail polish, sundresses. I refused to buy any more self-tanner.

Take something away from a person and you'll see their true colours. Without the tanner, she faded from deep orange right through to grey, and I noticed that underneath all that paint, underneath all that colour and distraction, she looked just like the one she loved most. The bulk of her was hanging off her bones now. Her hair was grey and frizzy, and she started wearing an old square pair of glasses that took up most of her face. She was covered in small curly hairs, on her arms, on her chin, even on her back.

I started to call her "Jer-een": "If Jer-een wants her sushi, she'll have to tell me what happened between her and Jerry," I'd say.

You have to understand, she had become so big, so persistent in her needs. You have to know, all that time I'd thought it was just the two of us.

WHEN THE SOUL leaves your body, you'll know. It was 8:27 on a Monday morning. The question, in a voice that gave me goosebumps: "After years of playing in the same configuration, why did Jerry and Phil one day decide to swap positions on stage?" I stammered, tried to cover it up with some good-natured banter, but the answer wouldn't come. I entered Laureen's room. Just as I expected, she was sitting up in bed with the radio off and the phone to her ear. I got down on my knees, pleading silently for the answer, but she just sat there with a crooked smile on her face, fat and happy. Her arms were folded across her chest, her mouth was tight, button-shaped.

While the station played all kinds of sound effects to mark the end of an era—applause, the opening of a vault, bottle rockets—I heard my own sound effects, a fizzle like one of those vitamin C tablets dissolving in water, then a small explosion, a pop really, a smell like a burnt raisin and a thin tuft of smoke. There goes my soul, I thought. I was no longer my own person. How does that proverb go? I was a man dreaming I was a dream dreamed by Laureen. I have to admit, down there, with the other parasitic life forms, out from under the burden of desire and free will—hunt and kill, catch and drag, the whole splashing and tugging mess of it— there was serenity.

SUMMER CAME ON hard, the hottest one on record. Rooftops sprung barbecues and the smell of roasting meat wafted in our windows day and night. Desperate for a tan, Laureen spent her days lying out in the full sun of our deck. Watching her struggle to turn over one day I decided, enough with retaliation. I would play the good husband. I would kill her with kindness, if that's what it took. From then on I oiled and flipped her at regular intervals. She turned the colour of tea with milk—slight freckling on her nose, arms, shoulders. Then amber ale—so many freckles it was difficult to see between them. Then the rich brown of a chestnut— freckles joining together—until, eventually, she was just one big, leathery freckle. Every night I propped her limbs, moisturizing and admiring her skin: the way it radiated the heat of the sun late into the night, salty lines running down her back like ocean currents seen from a plane, a million tiny wrinkles fanning out at each joint.

Every once in a while I'd taunt her—"If Jer-een wants a drink, she'd better fess up about that miracle"—but otherwise I was the perfect husband.

I EVENTUALLY GOT it out of her. It happened at a show in '86. Jerry'd just returned to the stage after coming out of a coma and the band was having a bad run. This show was no different. Jerry was forgetting words, fat, clumsy fingers on the guitar as though he was half sunk, pushing against water. Not only that, he seemed resentful, as if he blamed the audience for all that had happened to him.

Halfway through the set, Laureen, a teenager by this point, split off from the group. She'd been waiting in the Porta-Potty line but, giving up on that, had managed to find a narrow opening below the stage. While she was peeing all over the fat wires in that dark underworld, Jerry stormed away in the middle of the set. Laureen was still bent double, struggling to pull up her pants when someone lifted a panel in the floor and climbed down. She caught a brief glimpse of the man before he closed the panel; he was burly, really packed into his skin with curly hairs rising off every part of him. She heard him grunt and lie down at her feet, exactly where she'd just peed. He smelled of sweat and vinegar and he vibrated with tension. "Fuckin' bullshit, man," he said. "Can't fuckin' get 'em off." While the rest of the band struggled on above, Laureen did the only thing she thought she could; she leaned close to tell the man he was lying in a puddle of her pee. But before she had a chance, while she was still figuring out if it was more polite to say *urine,* he closed his eyes and began his confession. "Listen" he said, "there's just a few things I gotta get off my chest..." He told her he'd been juicing too much, that he was on a bummer, that things were getting heavy and he kept falling into the space between the notes. Then he told her about the coma, about walking through the valley of the shadow of death and having to choose, having to find one reason. When she finally realized who she was talking to, she said the words just came to her, she didn't know from where. Jerry and Laureen whispered back and forth to each other, two voices in the dark, for at least three songs. Then, near the end, something started to happen, the two of them saying the same things at the same time, as though their minds were one. It was so powerful, so tangible, neither one of them could let go of the feeling. "Meet me at the next show," he said before crawling away to play the last song. And they did. They met at the next show and the one after that and every other show for the rest of the tour.

"What'd you say to him? What'd he say back? Was it love? Was it magic? Was it wonderful?" I asked that first night I heard the story, and every night afterwards.

But whatever passed between Jerry and Laureen stayed between them. All I would ever know was the trivia: that there were ten years of letters living in shoeboxes in my closet; that, in a silent nod to what had happened under the stage that summer, the band's next album was called "In the Dark."

IS IT SO HARD to believe two people can become one, that a person can stop existing, just plug into someone else for a while? The Dead made a career of it, picking up cues from each other across space, changing tempo and keys, jamming seamlessly from one song to another. When they first started playing together, the two drummers used to sit shoulder to shoulder during practice. Like a two-headed monster with Shiva limbs waving, they learned to bang out rhythms with just a drumstick each, until one man's left and another man's right achieved total syncopation.

Most people can't imagine a love like this. Just like most people can't imagine why so many reasonable people hopped on buses and criss-crossed this country in the wake of a rock band, or the way, at a really good show, energy would flow back and forth, or that the jam came from the people as much as the band, that something was always shared the way it can only be shared in a family. But trivia can't teach you about a thing like that. It has to go through you.

Another thing trivia won't tell you: suicide isn't always announced with a siren wail or the crunch-pop of pills over linoleum. It can come on slow, over a year or a lifetime. It can wear the guise of food or drink, drugs or love. And you can smell it—sickly sweet like compost or coconuts gone bad—long before you recognize it.

Before she went, Laureen pulled me close and whispered last instructions: she wanted to be devoured; she wanted the letters made available to the family; she wanted to be worshipped—her life put to good use. She opened her eyes, said *please* and *I love you* and then she tried to say something else, something starting with *J*, and it may have been Jenson or Jet or even Jerry, but we'll never know because she died with that sound barely formed on her lips. She quivered then, and shrank in my arms, her skin hanging low and loose off her body like a deflated balloon. For a moment I thought I could see the shape of the old Laureen sinking under all that flesh, and then, because I was nothing, just a

LOVESEAT

ghost of a man, I was swept down and into that black hole of hers. Again a new language; I whimpered and kissed her skin while she groaned and breathed on and on, out and out, like a slow-leaking air mattress. Again three days in which I held her and became her. Three days to learn the miracles of the body, and of the bright still organs, and of the heart, slippery like a grape and too soft for this world.

THE GUYS I found were mostly immigrants, mostly illegal. Mario the butcher. Multiple generations in the business and yet, in this country, he couldn't get certified, so he got set up in a barn on the edge of town and learned to say yes to every kind of work—off-season game and more complicated jobs too. We sipped Cinzano on a couple of overturned buckets in the chill of his workshop, and I asked him, did he ever look at the living and see what they would become, was he ruined by what he did?

An old leather tanner named Yosef—guy with a moustache like you wouldn't believe. We stayed up late drinking clear liqueur that tasted like burnt hair while he told me about his best work, a yellowing hide pegged to the wall above us, a piece he'd tanned with such care, making sure to keep every freckle and detail in the skin. He'd tanned it in the old country the old way, rubbing the brains into the skin to begin the process. *Eet adds the peer-son-ality to the skeen,* he said, and his moustache jounced and bounced in such a way that I couldn't help but mouth the words along with him.

An upholsterer named Jesus. Together we picked our way through his shop, a graveyard of chairs waiting to be stuffed and covered. We passed a yerba mate gourd back and forth while he helped me choose a little loveseat.

I want you to know that technically, it's a double-wide chair, but I call it a loveseat because I'm a romantic and this is a love story. You should see the leather, so well-worn and gentled that it's transcended itself, the way the paper of an old map can come to feel like something else over time. And you should see how, when I step away, the leather of this loveseat remembers my shape, how it waits for my return. Day after day I sit here, looking out at the Baja coastline, thinking of her, snoozing the days of my early retirement away. Day after day I broadcast my story at the outer edges of the shortwave dial. Sometimes I have visitors, lovers and dreamers who've heard my story and made their way to the end of this long and bumpy road to see for themselves. They pay their money and I let them sit on my loveseat with the box of letters. There are some who find me cruel, some who question what I've done, but that's because they can't imagine a love like this. Sometimes, in the moments before or just after sleep, I can hardly imagine it myself.

large garbage

THEY'LL COME at night, the papers warned. They'll come hauling carts of empty wine bottles, all racket and ruckus, their skin the colour of city, the smog rubbed right in. They'll have no hygiene, no fixed address, no shoes or toothbrushes. Some will have no teeth. They'll come with their sores and their fleas and their nineteenth-century coughs, hacking and spitting, scratching and bleeding, right into our gardens and backyard gazebos. Like disease they'll come, fast and unforgiving.

"A new breed of homeless. A sign of the new economic reality," the experts claimed, although it meant little to us at the time. We knew they were overeducated, unemployed and migrating, east to west, across the country; we'd heard rumours of how they set up at the edges of wealthy neighbourhoods, living off the fat of the land, hosting late-night salons in other people's living rooms, but we all had our own economic realities to contend with. Some of us had even been forced to lay off the help.

At some point we stopped reading the stories. Sure, we fit the profile: a pocket of stately homes just at the edge of downtown, but our city was the westernmost in the country, set apart from the mainland by a two-hour stretch of ocean. We knew the last mainland city had been overrun, but we never believed they would find their way here, to our island, our city, our Cherry Lane. After all, we convinced ourselves, how would they afford the ferry fees?

MY WIFE, my daughter, and I were seated in the formal dining room when they arrived. Ever since we'd let Lucinda go, my wife, Kathy, had been doing the cooking. She liked to separate our carbs from our proteins, so that night it was all carbs: linguine with some sort of seed sprinkled on top and a side of pale, delicate potatoes.

"Would this be a fingerling potato?" I asked mere seconds before they appeared outside our window.

At first there were only two. He wore a tattered tuxedo and pushed a cart filled not with empty bottles, but with books. She was wearing mermaid-green taffeta, pearls and heels. The shoes were shaped like playground slides and not quite her size, so she weaved and wobbled like a child playing dress-up. There was a certain aura about them—not the mix of sex and decay I'd expected, but something almost noble, as if they'd been plucked from another time. They were both wearing pink sun-halos. Even the sunset had been recruited for this, their arrival scene.

My fingerling tumbled onto my plate, scattering seeds everywhere. My wife nodded to my daughter, then me, and we rose, moving to the window to watch the newcomers zigzag from the mouth of one driveway to the next, opening our recycling bins, the sturdy kind with wheels and lids. *Creak-slap* went those flip-top lids. Then the frenzied sifting—paper against paper against plastic.

"It's happening," my daughter, Jennifer, said, the small envelope of her lips quivering, a certain mosquito pitch rising in her voice.

It was all too much for my wife—who swooned beautifully, allowing me to steady her. Then I remembered the boxes I'd stacked in front of our garage the day before, once I saw the Gregorys had put theirs out, each one marked CHARITY in Lucinda's thick black writing.

"What about the Large Garbage?" I asked my wife, tight-lipped so she wouldn't see me tremble.

For some reason the residents of Cherry Lane had taken to calling the third week of September "Large Garbage Week," when we could just as easily have called it the Annual Charity Drive.

"I don't know why you insisted on putting that junk out so early," my wife said.

"Because the Gregorys did," I replied. "And the Felixes."

"The *Greg*orys did because they left for *Flor*-i-da today," she said. "And the *Fe*lixes did because *you* did." When she was smarter than me in a particular matter she enunciated very clearly.

The three of us leaned toward the window then, holding our breath, but it was too late. The strangers were tearing at boxes, emptying them of clothing, holiday placemats and old bedsheets. We looked at the tangle of high chairs, dismantled bunk beds, retro skis and tennis rackets stacked up in front of our neighbours' garages, all the things we unearthed from basements and attics each September to prove our charity to ourselves and to each other. "One man's treasure" and all that.

"Constantine," the woman called out from alongside our house, voice like a pencil scribble. "This one's a veritable jackpot."

"Constantine?" my wife said.

"Veritable?" I said.

But by then Constantine had discovered Mrs. Felix's box of books. "Proust!" he shouted, fanning the yellow pages. "Pinky, come see!"

"Pinky?" my daughter laughed. "More like *Skanky.*"

"Enough!" my wife commanded.

"What did we even put *out* there this year?" my daughter whined. "Anything of mine?" Her voice had risen to a whinny. "Mom, you can't just let them—"

"Why not?" I said. "Charity is charity."

"But I don't want to *see* it," Jennifer said.

My wife let down the blind. I turned up the chandelier and we guided our Jennifer back to the table.

"Never you mind," I said, putting my hand atop my daughter's, a wink for my wife. "Now, what can you tell me about the tenth grade?"

"Eleventh," she corrected. Although my error made them both momentarily glum, they soon recovered themselves.

While my daughter talked about her newest elective, Money Management, and the horrors of a certain partner named Hez, we could hear them outside, hooting and clattering, hauling boxes down driveways.

"Your grandfather on *my* side made his fortune in money management," my wife was telling Jennifer. "Foreclosures, refinancing, loss mitigation..." Jennifer was practically gurgling with excitement.

I tried to follow their conversation, but I'd heard it all before. Kathy was always delineating sides—hers, mine; good, bad; old money, no money. Besides, I was elsewhere. I was stabbing and twisting up bite-sized nests of linguine, trying to recall my own Proust days. My Balzac and Sartre and Camus days in the department of comparative literature, before Kathy persuaded me to switch to the school of business. I was arranging those pasta nests side by side on my plate because the appetite had gone right out of me, or rather it had shifted farther down to become something that had very little to do with food. The truth is, I couldn't quite recall what was in those boxes. In my race to keep up with the Gregorys, I hadn't even opened them.

I sat back in my chair, one hand fogging up my glass of Merlot, gripping the edge of my mahogany table, trying to take comfort in the largest room of my—our—large, large home. Antique cabinets, upholstered chairs, cut crystal: everything so finely crafted. Everything so sturdy, and yet I couldn't help but see myself as the most tender inside part of that life: me as mincemeat, as mollusc, as morsel.

IN THE MORNING, charity was strewn across our lawns. Clothing clogged gutters and hung from tree branches. Old magazines and once-loved toys cluttered the sidewalks. I was standing underneath the "two hours max at all times" sign, untucking parking tickets from my windshield wiper—one of the disadvantages of living so close to the city—and taking in the damage when I heard a chattering from under our hydrangea. I crept closer. It was tuxedo man, Constantine, reading—no, *reciting*—something to Pinky beneath a canopy of flowers. For a moment I envisioned them curled just so under a bridge in a large mainland city, inhaling exhaust fumes, scavenging for fish in diseased rivers, munching on gristly berries by the sides of highways. I felt a sudden kick of pride for having provided a downtrodden man with a flowering bush to sleep beneath—after all, it was *my* bush he'd chosen—and for a moment I longed for true charity, something beyond Large Garbage once a year. I imagined bringing this man into my home, giving him a shower and a shave, perhaps an old suit and a rudimentary lesson in entrepreneurship. Or if he wasn't interested in that, at least a proper fishing rod, some bait and tackle.

But this line of thought came to its snarled end when I noticed the woman was wearing something long, white and glittery, something familiar and poofy, and then it hit me: this skank was wearing my wife's cotillion gown. I could see it then. How, in my zeal to best the Gregorys, I'd not only grabbed the boxes marked CHARITY, but also those marked KEEPSAKES.

"Hey," I shouted, coming across the flowerbed at them. And I kept on, "Hey-hey. Hey. *Hey*," until I was close enough to reach out and grab Pinky. That's when I realized I didn't actually want to touch her.

The man stood and faced me. Now he was reading to me from the open book: *"Étonnants voyageurs. Quelles nobles histoires."* French: I flinched. I could barely tell one word from another these days. It was impossible not to hear his words as a personal insult.

"Nous lisons dans vos yeux profonds comme les mers," he continued. There I was, the enraged landowner, standing inside his orbit of stench and he could care less.

"Montrez-nous les écrins de vos riches mémoires…"

I recognized those words from a poem I'd once loved and was reminded of my leisurely undergraduate days, reading Baudelaire beneath trees. But I snapped out of it when I finally understood what was going on here—that I had also mistaken my own box of keepsakes for Large Garbage.

Something was rustling in the man's pants just then, and I looked down to see that he was scratching and rearranging himself *down there.* He was bouncing his meat at me. My gaze jolted back up to his face. Then his hand, the same one he'd used to scratch himself, was coming toward me. I could see his crumbling yellow nails, the grime built up in the creases of his palms. For a moment it seemed he would make some apologetic gesture, but then he opened his filthy crack of a mouth and said: "Would you happen to have any spare change?"

"No. No-no. No. No. No change. Sorry," I stuttered. I was a small angry man, a man of small anger. "This is our—*my* property and I command you to get *off,*" I hollered. "Go-go. Please go."

He didn't run as I had hoped but turned to offer his hand to Pinky.

She looked at the stack of parking tickets pinched in my hand. "You shouldn't park in front of your house anymore."

She was right, but ever since Kathy had given Jennifer a BMW (and my spot in the garage) for her sixteenth birthday, I'd had no choice.

"What was it the Marquis de Sade said?" She was wiggling into her heels. "'Social order at the expense of liberty is hardly a bargain.'" She stepped out from behind the hydrangea then, dainty as a debutante.

Constantine smiled. "Or, 'Miserable creatures, thrown for a moment on the surface of this little pile of mud,'" and then he looked at me just long enough to break the social contract. "You, sir, are you a miserable little creature?"

My mouth flapped: open, closed.

He threw his head back, laughing, and then they walked— no, sauntered—down my driveway. I didn't chase after them. I was stunned, speechless. And I was late. Again. As always.

I slammed into the car and headed for work, the previous night's parking tickets piled on top of all the others on the passenger seat beside me.

AT THE MINISTRY of Revenue I was hardly in the office door before man-faced Rhanda was on me.

"You're late," she said, and I couldn't help but notice in that particular light she really did have something like stubble. She was keeping pace with me down the hall, yapping and handing me memos. "The Schmidt case is being pushed ahead. Dan wants all the forms by noon. But he wants to talk to you first. ASAP. As soon as you're done with—" she looked at her clipboard—"Hez? Yes, Hez. She's waiting for you."

"Hez?"

"Hez. Your daughter's friend?"

"Deal with this, would you?" I said, handing Rhanda my dirty travel mug.

IT SEEMED THE little blonde princess Hez was there to talk to me about Money Management while my Jennifer was somewhere across town talking to Hez's father about the same thing. It seemed it was a competition of sorts. So I explained my position to her, then talked about taxation policy and departmental divisions and the various meetings I attended in any given week, but it wasn't good enough, somehow.

"Wait," she said. "So you don't manage any *actual* money?"

"I'm afraid it's not that simple," I said. "I'm more of an overseer really."

She waved her hand around. "So this is all just *files* and stuff? There's no actual *money* here? This office is more about paper pushing?"

"Well, Hez, I suppose it is," I said and then I gave her the number of my brother-in-law, the investment banker, before showing her out.

I stopped by Dan's office.

He squashed his blunt finger up against the Schmidt file, a couple of eighty-year-old artists who had managed to evade property tax for more decades than I'd been alive.

"Might I inquire when you were planning on dealing with them?" he did, indeed, inquire.

My tongue was fat and lazy in my mouth.

"Even the sweet and the old have to pay their taxes, Henry," he said, "but that's not what I really wanted to talk to you about." Looking grim, he pulled out another file, one I'd never seen before. "Well, Henry, in keeping with the new *Recession Measures Act,* our friends over in collections have given me a heads-up about your parking ticket situation." He cleared his throat. "Are you aware," he asked, "that you received a summons to go to court several weeks ago?"

I was not aware.

"And are you aware of the new ministry-wide zero-tolerance policy when it comes to matters of financial delinquency?"

I was not aware of that either.

"Jesus, Henry," he said, rising from his chair and looking about as sorry as a grown man can look, "if you'd come to me at any point, *any point* before now, we could have dealt with this reasonably. Like adults."

And so, in the end, it wasn't the Schmidts. In the end it was the parking tickets. Dan insisted that within the office, my "termination" would be strictly referred to as a "leave of absence." He insisted I would receive a respectable severance package.

On the way out the door I saw Rhanda gossiping by the copy machine. *Hiss-hiss-hiss,* she was saying, while glancing over her shoulder at me, which is why I was inclined, against my own better judgment, to walk right up to her and rustle my own pants. One minute I was heading for the door and the next I was thrusting up while reaching down. I was scratching and rearranging and jiggling my bits at her. I was calling her "a man-faced skank."

CHERRY LANE WAS still, except for a small fleet of charity vans idling by the curb. I hadn't been home at that time on a Monday for decades. The "hybrids"—as the media were now calling them—had gotten into the rest of the Large Garbage while everyone was at work. I stood on my doorstep watching the staff recover items from under bushes, off lawns and out of gutters. Where's the money management in this? I wondered. How exactly can these people afford to be volunteers in this day and age? I briefly considered helping but I was overdrawn, expired.

I called to my wife and daughter from the foyer, but it was just me, *man alone.* I instinctively went to the den, kicked off my shoes and clicked on the TV, but it was hours until prime time. I turned it off and that's when I caught a whiff coming from the couch pillows. It was gamey, oniony, slightly animal—a smell some part of me enjoyed, but a smell that had no place in my home. I lifted a pillow to my face and sniffed deeply. I must've drifted away for a time then, for I woke in the afternoon with that pillow sitting on my face, smelling more scalpy than ever.

I sat up with a start and noticed that all of the couch pillows were mussed, that the carpet was showing signs of heavy traffic—and yet, since Lucinda had left, my Kathy had been so diligent, one might even say obsessed, with these kinds of things. She was always making sure the carpet pile went the same way.

I went from room to room then, sniffing, checking the window locks.

In the kitchen I found cheese and cracker crumbs. Cheese *and* crackers: carbs *and* protein. Upstairs, in the master bathroom, I found a bar of soap with deep, dark striations where dirt had settled in. There was a faint scum line around the perimeter of the tub, as though several dirty bodies had been washed there. Glued against the porcelain was a curly red hair. I was searching my wife's drawer for tweezers to collect the hair when I happened to glance out the window and see more hybrids, seven or eight of them, making their way slowly through the ravine at the back of our property. The men were wearing ratty suits and top hats, the women fur and silk.

Never mind tweezers. I was hauling down the stairs with that hair pinched between my fingers when my wife and daughter stepped into the foyer.

"Thank God you're home," I shouted and then my feet kicked out from under me and I slid down the last few stairs.

They were giggling in their matching yoga wear and the hair escaped my pinch.

"They've been in here," I said. "Those homeless people. I just found a hair in the tub."

"*Gross*, Dad!" Jennifer said.

"I think they've been taking baths."

They looked at me blankly then, all the giggle gone out of them.

LARGE GARBAGE

"Well, maybe you should have considered this before you let Lucinda go," Kathy said.

"No, not *our* hair," I said. "One of theirs. A red one. Wait, I'll show you." I was patting the floor around me. I was pleading, "C'mon. Help me look."

"I've got homework," Jennifer said.

"I've got dinner," Kathy said, holding up a grocery bag and then they split off—north, south—and I headed for the computer.

THAT NIGHT it was all protein: breast of something covered in sauce with a peculiar sausage as a side. The blinds were snapped tight but we could still hear them out there.

"You know they're calling them hybrids now?" I said. Then in my best newscaster voice: "'The *New* Hybrid Class.'" I was the only one laughing. "They're really quite educated," I added.

Neither Kathy nor Jennifer had a response—just the sounds of chewing, scraping, swallowing.

My fork was poised somewhere between plate and mouth when I noticed the sauce was made from the finest paper-thin slices of mushroom. "What type of mushroom is this?" I asked.

"Chanterelle," Kathy answered.

"Such a lovely word," I said, to kill the silence. Meanwhile, I was wondering how, exactly, was I different from this mushroom? I ate, I slept, I too grew larger, paler by the day.

Eyes on plates. Sipping, slicing, clinking of ice.

"Apparently they were once middle class," I said. "They were students, artists, professor types, too-good-for-the-corporate-ladder types. And when they couldn't afford their passions anymore, they just . . . dropped out."

"Like your father!" Kathy said to her dinner plate.

"Passion," I said to mine. "Another lovely word!"

I persisted. "Evidently they've been holding 'salons' in people's homes. If a family is away, for instance, they'll just go right in and read all their books and hold seminars. Apparently property values have really . . ."

But I was speaking to myself. They were involved in some sort of mother-daughter communication requiring only the slightest eyebrow movements.

Kathy put her fork down, folded her arms across her chest and looked at me. My daughter, having missed her cue, joined in at the folding-of-the-arms part, fork still in hand.

I looked from my daughter to my wife: *my Jennifer, my Kathy.* It was what one might call an awkward silence.

A slice of chanterelle fainted from my fork, fell to my plate.

"What did you do to Hez?" Jennifer said finally.

"And how is it you can afford to be home from work so early?" Kathy asked.

I was still formulating a response when a bright, farm-smelling whiff passed my nose. "Do you smell that?" I asked, louder than I meant to, so loud Kathy startled. "That funny smell? Like a greasy scalp? I'm telling you, they've been in here!"

I DECIDED TO tell my wife about the tickets that night. Just the tickets. I figured I'd get to the termination thing a little later. She was on the bed rubbing lotion on her legs.

"How many tickets?"

"Oh, I don't know," I said, "twenty, forty. It's nothing really."

"Forty!" she screeched. She rubbed more vigorously then, going over the same area again and again—now knees, now ankles, now knees-knees-knees.

"I'd planned to dispute them when I had a moment. I mean, they can't give a man fifty tickets for parking in front of his own house! They can't just declare Cherry Lane a two-hour-max-anytime zone. 'Social order is hardly worth the price of liberty.' You know who said that?"

"Now it's fifty tickets?"

"What?"

"A minute ago it was forty tickets. Now it's fifty?"

I pulled back my side of the sheet and looked closely at the accumulation of bodily crumbs there. I couldn't, just then, be certain they were my own.

"I think the den needs vacuuming," I said.

"I think you're more and more like your father every day," she said.

"I think I'll be taking a flex day tomorrow," I said, and then I headed for the couch downstairs.

IN THE MORNING there was no sign of them, not behind the hydrangea and not in the ravine either. I headed for the basement and, as I'd feared, found two boxes marked CHARITY among those marked KEEPSAKES. Most of the keepsake boxes were Kathy's: the Montgomery linens tucked in with the Montgomery china and the Montgomery photo albums—boxes of dresses and shoes and ribbons and trophies for every occasion in a Southern girl's life. In among all that was a single box marked KEEPSAKES: BROWN. My family inheritance. I brought it out to the backyard.

I found six of my father's journals. The first one was from the France years, just after his PhD and just before my mom. It was written in scratchy black French. French: the language I could read and write but never quite speak, a taunting, cruel language, a language that had led me right up to the threshold of fluency and then shut the door on me. I almost broke down. I did. My tears landed on the open page, drawing the ink up from the page, the page up from the book. I dabbed with my shirtsleeve but I was only smearing ink and history. I almost gave up, and then the sentences I was reading began to loosen. Verbs and their conjugations, nouns and their complements, tense, vocabulary: it all started rushing back to me as if French, like a good woman, had been waiting for me all those years, as if no time had passed at all.

I read verse after verse about *la lune,* about grass blowing in the wind, women's hair blowing in the wind, hair luminous and flowing and silky and honey-coloured. Rivers of hair. Entire poems about a woman's eyes. Eyes like syrup, no, coffee, no, caramel, no, amber. The eyes of a seductress. Tantalizing, come-hither eyes. Page after page about a woman's curves, vast swells of flesh, heaving mountains, soft veldts, damp crevasses.

I closed the book. It was my mother, of course.

My dear father. He had the heart of a poet but not the talent, which is why he'd devoted his life to the study of troubadours. One of only a handful of troubadour scholars at the time, he had gone to France to walk in their footsteps, to dig through archives and write a book about his findings. It was while researching a certain French family and their history of troubadour patronage that he met the man who would be my grandfather, and his daughter, who would be my mother. My father was a scruffy American with a big nose and corduroy pants, but my grandfather was so impressed by the young man's interest in history he let his daughter marry him anyway. So began the Brown family tradition of "marrying up."

My father wrote the book, but not before one of his colleagues did, so he was always given second pick of the jobs and the conferences. He worked in a small, cluttered office at the local university until my mother left him—and who could blame her? He had begun to dress in head-to-toe brown as so many scholars do, but, given our name, it made him a target for ridicule. He would wear the same shirt-pant-cardigan combination until it was sour smelling, at which point he would change the shirt or the pants, never both. He smoked and drank with his friends, scholars of equally obscure subjects: *Fifteenth-Century Swords of the Middle East, Italian Rococo Hairstyles* and *Ceilings of Rajasthan.* And he wrote terrible French poetry.

AFTER HOURS OF sitting in the grass reading my father's writing, I saw Constantine stroll into my yard.

"Hello," he said, not bothered in the least by our trespasser–landowner relationship.

"Hi." I couldn't seem to locate anger.

"What is the meaning of this?" He gestured at the clutter around me. I noticed he was covered in a noble grime.

"Reorganizing," I said, closing the box.

He gave an aristocratic shrug—the first sign of approval I'd had from anyone in days.

"I'm going to have to ask your girlfriend for that dress back. The white one."

"That seems reasonable," he said.

I nodded toward the sandwich in his hand. "What's that?"

He cracked the bread open. "Prosciutto, brie, tapenade—"

"Is that grilled portobello?"

"It appears to be," he said, and ripped off a mouthful. Then he held the sandwich out to me, "Care for some?"

We shared the sandwich and a bit of conversation. Eventually he excused himself to look for my wife's dress, and I carried my box inside. It was then, just after he had left, that I managed to locate my anger after all. Where exactly did a hobo like him get a sandwich like that? Just who did he think he was, breaking into the kitchens of the good people of Cherry Lane? I was starting to think laying Lucinda off was one of the greatest mistakes of my life—Lucinda, not just the maid, but the guardian of our home—when I noticed a stiff wind, the front door standing wide open and more of that deep-skin smell. Only this time, it was everywhere.

I found body-shaped ruts down the centre of each bed, grease spots as dark as cheeseburger stains on the pillow-cases. The bottom bookshelf, down where we kept our Joseph Campbell and Carl Jung, was in disarray. In the living room, the chess set had been hastily put back on the shelf. The TV was on *Masterpiece Theatre*. The radio was tuned to NPR.

LARGE GARBAGE

AFTER I TOLD her about the mix-up with her keepsakes, and the trouble at work, and after she dragged my father into it and I dragged her mother into it, Kathy suggested I spend the night at a hotel. I chose to stay in the yard, though, where I could keep an eye on things.

I spent the early part of that evening reading my father's journals, falling deeper into French than I ever imagined I could, the language opening to me in new ways. At the bottom of the box, beneath the journals, I found my father's old scholarly uniform: brown pants, brown cardigan, brown shirt and tie, all my size. Putting those clothes on, I understood why my father wore them a week at a time; it's a quality you just don't find in clothes anymore.

The uniform must've filled me with strength and purpose, because I immediately got an idea. After writing out twelve versions of the same note, I walked up and down Cherry Lane tucking one into every mailbox. The notes were a call to action: *Tomorrow, 5 pm, my yard, be there,* or something to that effect. Then I got the idea to keep an eye on the Gregorys' house from inside the bushes.

It was nearly midnight when I heard them. I climbed out of the bushes in time to see a dim, shifty light, a candle or a Bic lighter, moving through the Gregorys' house. I crept across the yard, on hands and knees, and pulled myself up against the tall fence separating our yards. I could smell tuna grilling. I could hear the clink of wineglasses, the hot tub bubbling.

I didn't even walk around the fence; I jumped over and marched up the back steps to confront those hybrids for once and for all.

There were ten, fifteen, twenty of them. They were in the yard, on the porch, in the house. The ones in the patio hot tub were nude, debating intensely. Inside, the air was thick with cigar smoke. It was dark but for the moon and the odd candle. My clothes must've helped me blend in, because nobody noticed me at first. In the living room women and men were lounging about, sipping wine with their feet in each other's laps. They were passing a book—Rilke? Neruda?—taking turns reading verses aloud. The last woman to read finished the poem and asked, "What do you think it means?" closing the book gently. "Do you think he might really fail his lover or is he just afraid of his own mortality?" I was tempted to lie down with them, to speak about love and death while some young woman played with my hair, but I kept on.

Several people were gathered around the dining room table, attempting to interpret a tide chart. They had an almanac out, an atlas, a dictionary, a small flashlight. A petite redhead was at the kitchen counter dishing out food. "Niçoise?" she offered each passerby. It smelled delicious.

A man was drawing different constellations into the dust of the foyer mirror. Cassiopeia, Pegasus and Chamaeleon: he described each one and then a huddle of women with tall hairstyles and names like Scarlett and Arabella recreated the shapes by squeaking their fingers across the marble floor.

On the stairs, two men in tailcoats were debating the Bible from a literary standpoint. "From a purely literary standpoint, Genesis almost directly correlates to Aristotelian structure," one said as I passed. In the upstairs hallway a couple was slow dancing to a song only they could hear. They were humming softly, voices in perfect harmony. Another couple was making love in the spare bedroom. I stopped before the open door. "You complete me!" the man yelled. "You com*plete* me!" and then they collapsed in groans. A woman smelling of snuffed-out fires came up beside me and passed me an orb filled with bright smoke. I inhaled once, twice, and began to feel impaled. Then, once I was a limbless black core, once I was only the body, only the parts of me that beat, she led me toward the master bedroom. Pinky was there, and Constantine. He was playing a delicate stringed instrument (a lyre?) and she was warbling operatically. They were accompanied by a woman playing some sort of pan pipe.

People were twirling and floating around the room in what can only be described as interpretive dance. The woman, my friend, led me forward and before I knew it my arms were swaying—now I was a tree, now a woman's hair, now grass in the wind. I was twisting carpet pile up between my toes like meringue and reciting something, a French poem I had memorized years ago, a poem I forgot I knew.

I WOKE UP late, alone on Bruce and Linda Gregory's bed, my mouth coated in red wine, salade niçoise ground into my hair. Except for a few minor details—couch pillows, crumbs, the odd carpet blemish—the house had been put back in order.

It was afternoon. Driveways stood empty and for a moment I thought my wife had locked me out accidentally until I found a stack of sandwiches and a glass of milk set outside the back door. There were three, peanut butter and jam, carbs and protein, hastily thrown together. I ate all three, one after another. Then I revised my notes in preparation for the meeting.

At five o'clock on the dot the neighbours filed into the backyard. They arranged themselves along familiar lines—the Andersons clustered next to the Smiths next to the Woodwards, families waving to families across polite distances.

I cleared my throat and mentioned that I'd been keeping an eye on the hybrids. "We all know they're sleeping beneath our shrubbery," I said, "but did you know they are also living inside our houses while we're at work?"

Alarmed murmurs.

"You may not detect the signs at first," I said, "but I suggest sniffing your pillows, checking the backs of bookshelves for volumes of poetry, philosophy, literary criticism. I suggest steaming up your mirrors and looking for messages written there."

They were whispering among themselves and I was beginning to sense skepticism.

"Now you might wonder how it is I know this," I said. "The truth is, I infiltrated one of their 'salons' last night, and what I found was rather fascinating. The funny thing is—" I tried to chuckle, but it worked itself into a frog, then a rattle, then a nineteenth-century cough. "The funny thing is," I tried again, "I think these people may have something to offer. I think, when you find these clues I've mentioned, you might also encounter parts of yourself, long-forgotten parts: books you always meant to read, little notes you scribbled to yourself years ago. You might ask yourself, 'Who was I

before all of this?' and 'When did *that* end and *this* begin?'
You might reassess, I mean *really* reassess, and change your
priorities. And you might start to wonder, 'Who's really free,
us or them?'"

"Where's Kathy?" Mrs. Park asked.

"She'll be home any minute," I said.

"Why are you dressed like that?" one of the teenagers
asked. Snicker, snicker went the rest.

"Well, I'm locked out and I haven't had a chance to—"

"You're locked out?" someone asked.

"Of your own house?" said someone else.

"What exactly is going on with you, Henry?"

"Hold on now. Hold on just a minute." I was that movie
actor from *It's a Wonderful Life,* overly earnest, trying to control the angry mob. "I gathered you here to tell you about—"

"How long have you been living in the backyard, Henry?"
someone interrupted.

"Wait,"—it was one of the teenagers—"didn't I see you
sharing a sandwich with one of them yesterday?"

"You're getting this all wrong. This isn't about me. This is
about our community and our way of life—"

Just then the back door opened. It was Kathy, home from
work, and she was ushering the neighbours in the door. Like
a funeral procession, each family stopped and whispered
their apologies before entering my house. I brought up the
back of the line. I whispered an apology too even though I
wasn't sorry for anything, not really.

"You stay here," she said, her palm open on my chest. "I
need some time." Her eyes travelled up and down my body,

taking in my outfit. "Jesus, Henry," she said and then shut the door on me. I heard the twist of the lock.

An hour later the neighbours filed out. I could hear them out front—one bright goodbye after another—but I didn't go around. I waited by the back door until the sky grew dark from the east and the mosquitoes rose from the ravine. I waited for Kathy until the bedroom lights came on and moths clunked against the windows.

"Jennifer," I called up in a loud whisper, but she must've already been asleep.

I moved to the other window. "Kathy? Kathy?"

Finally a Kathy-shaped shadow came to the window, her triangle of hair, her small sad shoulders. *My wife.*

"Honey, I understand you're mad at me, but could you spare a little change? Just a little?"

But she quickly moved away.

THE NEXT MORNING there were only two sandwiches—no peanut butter, just marmalade—and water instead of milk. I tried to remember the previous day's joy, but I was dirty and hungry and the tiny hairs of my beard were curling back on me.

I was working on a poem, something to move Kathy to forgiveness, when I heard the bright chirp of teenage-talk coming from the yard next door—not the Gregory side, but the other side.

I moved to the fence. I heard something about Jennifer first, some new boy she was dating. He was *way* better than her, they said; she was *totally* lucky. *That's my Jennifer,* I thought, *dating up!* Then their talk turned to me. Kathy was divorcing me, they said. I had lost my mind and my job and my wife all in one week.

I considered bribing them for entrance to their house. I could've finagled a shower and a shave probably, maybe even one of their dad's suits. I could've headed downtown, talked to Dan and apologized to Rhanda, begged for my job and fit right back into my old life, but I didn't. Instead I poked my head over the fence.

"Excuse me," I said. "When you say Jennifer's boyfriend is better, do you mean from a wealthier family or just more popular?"

They were frozen on the spot, baring their braces at me.

"Listen," I said, "I won't tell your parents you're skipping school if you give me some change. Just enough for a hamburger. And a coffee."

WHEN JENNIFER and Kathy got home later that evening, I was ready. I gave them a moment to get settled, to turn on some lights. Then I stood in the gazebo and yelled to the house. First, an invitation: "My daughter and my wife, my love and my life, please listen to what I have written. Please let me in my home. Please don't leave me out here alone." I saw their heads in the window and then I began to recite in my best approximation of French: *"La lune, la lune…"*

IT RAINED that night, so I was forced to sleep in the shed between the lawnmower and the weedwacker. I could hear the hybrids in the distance. They were chanting something sounding like *heave-ho,* or *hobo,* or *let's go.* I read until I slept. I cried until my face was plastered to the pages of my father's diary.

I ATE THE LAST sandwich in the early morning, looking back at my house from the middle of the yard. This time it was only butter, stale bread, no drink. I knew what the next day would bring. I didn't want to be there to see it.

I looked at the building that had contained my life for so many years. Brick and mortar, wood and glass. I thought of my life inside those walls: a kind of mushroom sleep, happiness like a heavy lid. I tried to remember my wife as soft, the contours of her body, but all I could think about were bones, sinew, digestion, respiration—the materials and mechanisms that held her together. I noticed a place where the shingles had lifted off above the sunroom and it was as if I could see the future. There would be a leak in that spot soon. At night my wife and daughter would lay their cheeks in someone else's hair grease and dream of money and acquisition and accomplishment. Other people would read their books and sleep in their beds and Kathy and Jennifer would be forced to buy zit zappers and special creams to cure their mysteriously oily cheeks. They would buy air fresheners to cover the strange goat smells they sometimes found and they would straighten their bookshelves again and again, never knowing what went on while they were away because only a few ever do. Only a few are brave enough to admit that we're all living off each other, one way or another.

LARGE GARBAGE

Meanwhile, I am moving south with Pinky and Constantine and the rest of the hybrids. We enter people's homes and, while the others deplete the food and drink the wine and lather on expensive shampoos, I find a patch of sunlight to curl up in with a good woman—Pinky, or Scarlett, or Arabella—and she is wearing my father's sweater, and spooning me, wrapping me up in my father's brown sleeves, tugging me down, and my eyelids are filling with fire colours and I am drifting into dreams, dreams large enough to haunt the hollow rooms of another man's home, dreams of poetry and of history, of freedom and of motion. It is the future and I am right where I belong, dreaming troubadour dreams older than me.

mrs. english
teacher

AT FIRST IT'S about money, or its opposite—student debt, that big red wrecking ball swinging above your head at all times.

"So you can assure me the country is no longer at war?" you ask the recruiter before committing to a year.

"No war, promise," she says.

You sign and fax the contract the same day.

Then, for a brief time, it's about the adventure. "I could've chosen Tokyo or Dubai," you tell friends, "but I'm tired of safe." You have visions of twisty alleys, old women retreating into darkened doorways, spicy air, dusty sunsets. It's about leaving behind a peculiar kind of emptiness you've always associated with home—your lightweight life, like a hollowed-out shell.

At your going-away party your smart friend, the one writing a dissertation on everything that's wrong with the world, asks, "Don't you worry ESL teachers are just agents of modern colonialism?" So you spend your last nights at home worrying about exactly that, dreaming of angry white men preaching in tents in the middle of jungles. Then, finally, you stop to consider the source of all this doubt: your smart friend who refuses to shave her legs and bikes her dripping compost to her mother's house across town once a week, your smart friend who always speaks about her "footprint," who is in fact footprint-obsessed at the expense of romance and career opportunities. You recall the time she scolded you for whitening your teeth and decide, if anything, she is the one raging in the tent. If anything, you are the one out in the jungle holding hands with the children, singing fun and educational songs.

In the end you are grateful to your friend for exorcising your doubts, for helping you home in on what this trip is really about: a desire to do good in the world and a war-ravaged village that needs you. You write her to say thank you for the exorcism and that you will be sure not to leave a single footprint in this foreign land, other than those footprints you've actually been hired to leave. It is the last thing you do before takeoff, mailing that postcard from the airport.

SOON YOU ARE in the back of a van, queasy and sweating, being driven through the landscape you've imagined and reimagined for months. Everything is as expected: the blue-green Tolkien hills in the distance, at the foot of those hills the small, dust-coloured village you will call home. Everything looks exactly like the past. One-room houses with dirt floors and woven walls are scattered across the land like upside-down baskets. There are stray chickens and barefoot boys, goats and mules, men in fields leaning on shovels to grimace at the sky. They know it as well as you: somewhere beyond those hills there is a village flooding, a river slipping its banks, people drowning, mud bubbling. This is a country at the mercy of weather and war. Someone is always dying, but you feel more alive than ever.

The two men who met you at the airport hardly said hello. They nodded gruffly, said what sounded like "yuh-yuh" and helped you into the back of the van. Now they are seated up at the front, hardly watching the road, watching instead a small black-and-white TV wedged between the dashboard and window—old reruns of the same medical drama your father likes so much, the one where people are always making speeches over open bodies. The subtitles take up half the screen. This isn't much of a welcoming but you're too tired to be offended. There will be plenty of time to explain about handshakes and hugs, about receiving a home-cooked meal after a long flight.

The men carry your bags into your hut and leave. It is nothing like the picture the recruiter sent you. It has the ambience of a shed—a single room with a bare bulb hanging from the ceiling, a thin sliding metal door and concrete floors that slope toward a drain in the middle. When you shower, the water fans out across the floor. You have to run around swearing and dripping, dragging luggage to higher ground. That's when the note you scribbled earlier flutters out of your purse—*Embrace the exotic!* it says. You stick it to the wall above your bed, but it's already irrelevant. Already it seems written by another type of person.

The next morning you discover the school is nothing like its photo either. This school is smaller, less reliable looking. Every wall and window is plastered over with rusty old tin signage salvaged from the nearest city. The whole building seems to flap in the wind like a prehistoric bird. You are met by the principal, Mr. Bruce, a short, brisk man dressed for some reason like an Oxford don. He leads you up a long flight of stairs. Inside, the school is like a cave, hardly a sliver of daylight available. Each classroom has bare walls and a window looking onto the hallway. You and Mr. Bruce stop to peer into classes 1A, 1B and 1C. You are just about to suggest more imaginative names, something the students can identify with—dolphins or tigers—when a teacher slaps a ruler across her desk to call the class to attention. The students scurry like sand crabs, tucking limbs under desks. Mr. Bruce folds his hands behind his back and rocks forward onto his toes, looking pleased. As you move down the hall, you notice that the teachers are all women, all from this part of the world. None of them are teaching English *in* English, and for some reason all of the teachers and female students are wearing cloth masks over their noses and mouths.

You catch Mr. Bruce by the leather patch on his elbow. "Why do they wear these masks?"

He pauses, throws his head back, as if searching the ceiling of his mind. Then he nods and says, "Priacy," stabbing down with his chin.

You squint at his mouth. It's as if his face is too tight or his tongue is too short to speak clearly.

"Oh, *privacy!*" you say at last. But something must've been lost in translation. Clearly there is either a health concern or this is some form of female oppression. You can't imagine how wearing a tiny little mask offers a person any privacy.

IN HIS SMALL brown office, Mr. Bruce sits on the other side of his desk, beneath a framed poster of Bruce Lee, and explains that you will be given the school's "number one, top-prize class," the twelve oldest students who are closing in on the "X Test." He explains how long the students have been preparing, how far they must walk to class, how devastated they were when the last teacher quit just four months before the test, but you know all this because the recruiter prepped you. You also know Mr. Bruce means "exit test," a standardized exam divided into the areas of Speech and Writing, Vocabulary and Grammar—you have been brought in for Speech. You are the only native-speaking English teacher in the whole country, Mr. Bruce says, so your students have a great advantage. There appears to be a problem though, changes made to the testing format. It's all very troubling to Mr. Bruce, who is now spitting and shouting.

"X Test is eye of needle," he says, waving his hands over his head. "For this they working whole long life! Now big change!"

It's only once he slides a memo across his desk that you understand. It seems the test makers have decided to add an additional item to the Speech portion of the test. Students will now have to give a three-minute speech on what makes them unique.

"Oh, this is nothing," you say, sliding the memo back across his desk. "Piece of cake. I don't think we need to worry about this."

He looks puzzled. "But 'uniques,'" he says, jabbing his finger at the memo.

"Students love to talk about themselves," you say.

"But we have no uniques," he says. "Uniques is opposite of war."

That strikes you as profoundly true: soldiers and corpses *are* far from unique. "Yes," you say, "but the war is over and I'm confident each one of your students has a unique living inside them."

Mr. Bruce looks briefly reassured. He returns to his eye-of-the-needle speech, but you already know the drill: only the top two students in the country will be given the opportunity to attend an American university; of those left behind, only ten percent will gain entrance to the country's one university; for the rest, the exit test will mark the end of their education—the girls will marry and the boys will begin mandatory military service.

"Other side of needle," Mr. Bruce continues, "is Ha-vad." He nods fiercely.

"Harvard?" You laugh just a little, more of a snort really. Even your smart friend couldn't get into Harvard.

He fixes his eyes on your collarbone and flings his hand toward a portrait hanging on the wall behind you, saying, "See fo' self." The portrait is of a young man dressed in graduation regalia. It must've been taken in the seventies, the way his hair is feathered, the way he looks immersed in a soft purple fog. The table beneath the picture is done up like a shrine with fake flowers and bouquets of red and gold Harvard pencils, never sharpened.

"My student. Ha-vad grad," Mr. Bruce says. Then, as if offering you a mantra for the coming months, he says, "Havad, Ha-vad, Ha-vad." He is snapping down on the words, angry or rapturous or both.

WHEN YOU ENTER the classroom for the first time, your students are already seated, looking bored but determined, as if they've come to do your taxes. The boys and girls are on opposite sides of the room and the girls are all wearing those privacy masks.

When you smile, their faces scrunch up like babies encountering something bright or sour for the first time.

You attempt introductions but they all say the same thing—what sounds like "I am Pin Pon"—and you lose track. You can't tell if the girls are smiling or frowning behind their masks and the boys might as well be wearing them, their faces are so placid.

You write your name on the board, but it doesn't matter. You are "Mrs. Teacher" to them.

You notice that the boys have textbooks but no paper, that the girls have paper but no textbooks, so you ask them to pair up while you search for supplies. But by the time you find pencils nobody has moved and Principal Bruce is peering in through the hallway window.

All of this might be intimidating except that you believe Speech to be the most dynamic of subjects. With Speech there is no need for textbooks *or* pencils *or* paper. You will write a topic on the board and in no time at all the room will fill with the dull roar of opinion.

You break the class up into girl-girl, boy-boy teams and open your X Test book to find a topic. The first ones are all about extracurricular activities—TV and team sports and afternoons at the mall. The next ones are all about money—allowances, college funds and after-school jobs. You flip through the pages but the rest of the topics are no better. They're centred on the perils of modern North American life: obesity, skin cancer, drinking and driving.

You snap the book shut. "What would *you* like to make speeches about?" you ask brightly. You will be the fun teacher, like Robin Williams in that movie. In this room learning will be relevant, crucial, exciting.

The boys stare through you. The girls look at their hands.

"Things to do when not farming?"

No response.

"The perils of riding a bike with a flat tire?"

Still nothing.

"What to do during a mudslide?"

And that's when you sense it, a total lack of comprehension.

YOU DISCOVER YOUR students speak barely comprehensible English, that even though their vocabulary is excellent, English sounds like mashed potatoes in their mouths. Because their own language requires swallowing entire syllables, getting them to open their mouths and enunciate may be the single greatest challenge of your teaching career.

You draw larger-than-life pictures of the inside of a mouth, the tongue curling or backing up to make certain sounds. Then, to show Mr. Bruce the true meaning of privacy, you tape these pictures over the hallway window. Now when he stops to peer in, his head is a shadow perched on the tip of a huge tongue.

The first week is all about pronunciation. You lead them through a series of facial contortions while repeating "A-E-I-O-U" and the various diphthongs, but there's only so much progress you can make while the girls' mouths are behind masks. You have reason to suspect these masks are holding the boys back too, not to mention the country.

After work on Friday you corner Mrs. Diana, the only other teacher with even a smattering of English, and confirm via charades that indeed the masks have nothing to do with contagion, nothing to do with privacy. That's when you decide it: next week will be different.

"It's just, I've come all this way," you explain to Mrs. Diana, "and there are only four months until the test."

ON MONDAY MORNING the whole procedure takes only a few minutes. You get the boys to face the back wall and the girls to face you. There is some whimpering and the girls hang their heads for a time, but you try not to take that on. You do have to resort to the ruler twice, but it's all for the greater good. You are stripping them of their masks, true, but in exchange you are giving them the world.

You try to illustrate this point for them: "Do you think American women hide their mouths? Do you think you'll fit in at Harvard showing half a face?"

On the first day, the boys and girls continue to face away from each other while you run them through call-and-response speaking drills. On the second day, you hand out small mirrors and invite them to watch themselves talk. On the third day, when the girls raise their wet brown eyes to meet your own, it is like seeing them for the first time. Such trembling beauty! So many lovely differentiated mouths! These young women are blooming before your eyes, speaking with clarity and a new confidence.

You know it's finally time for the boys and girls to face one another when you catch them stealing glances at each other in their mirrors. It is awkward and heart-thumping at first. Their faces change colour and the heat rises in the room as they turn slowly, hands squeaking across desks. You cheer them on from the back of the room: "Freedom isn't for the faint of heart!" and "One day you'll thank me!"

At the end of each day, your students file past you before leaving the classroom. One by one the girls stop to tie their masks back on. You hold your finger to your lips, "Shhhh." Their eyes darken with understanding and then they step out into the hall.

Before long your students' mothers start gathering at the top of the stairs after school. They stand just beyond the front doors, whispering amongst themselves. You wave to them, but they don't wave back. You smile and they flinch. Their eyes slice at you—up-down, up-down. You feel naked—more than naked—you feel carved out.

BY THE END of your first month your students are ready for sentences. You hang noun and verb and adjective lists all over the walls of your classroom. You write "Subject Verb Object" on the board and then leap from one word list to another, guiding your students through the anatomy of a sentence. At times, standing at the front of class with your mouth stretched into a hideous yawn, waiting for a student to speak, you imagine the right word dangling on the end of a string way down inside you. If a student is really struggling, fishing around desperately for a word, you can feel it being tugged up through you. It scrapes your throat. You gag. Your tongue bucks and then, as if by magic, the word arrives fully formed in their mouths. You applaud, and then turn to wipe your eyes with your sleeve.

The more they speak, the more you sacrifice yourself, that old teacher's trick. "Describe me!" you instruct, and the sentences come rushing forward: Mrs. Teacher is ample/corpulent/spherical/abundant. According to one boy whose father is a dairy farmer, Mrs. Teacher is soft like cow belly. This is the day you write "taboo" on the board and give a short lecture—your first—about how people politely describe one another in America. They glom onto the word. Taboo: pronounced "ta-BOOH!" It makes them giggle every time.

Almost as soon as your students are speaking freely, something takes hold of your voice. You try to speak, but it snags at the back of your throat.

"It is bugs," Mr. Bruce says when he hears you coughing. In the past weeks the air has grown thick with them: gnats, no-see-ums and smaller bugs too. Walking home they coat your arms and legs. They form a thick bug-paste in the corners of your eyes.

"It's nothing," you tell Mr. Bruce. "Just a tickle."

IT'S THE END of your second month. You have given them sentence structure and vocabulary. You have given them voice and freedom, but your students still can't form opinions about any of the speech topics.

Your voice is reedy and thin now, but day after day you explain about American problems—about how hard it is for obese people to fit on airplanes, about all the high school students who drive drunk and all their angry mothers, about how people with melanoma have to get skin from their thighs grafted onto their noses. Night after night you ask them to form their own opinions about these things, but they always return empty-handed, saying only, "I think what you think, Mrs. Teacher."

Instead of American problems, they want to know about hotdogs and California and shopping malls with indoor roller coasters. You end up giving lengthy, sideways-sliding speeches. You start out talking about Disneyland and end up talking about tolerance, equality, democracy.

They always rein you in again though, interrupting to ask, "And what about ice cream? How many flavours?" or "And the shoes, even red ones?" or they jump up from their seats, cinching their pants tight around their legs, asking, "American jeans are even *this* much tight?"

You teach them the word *because* and they are suddenly speaking in long chains of logic that stretch away without end: *It is good to study English because it makes you smart. It is good to be smart because you go to Harvard.* Still you have to tell them what to say on either side of *because*.

"Harvard is good because—" They stop, look up at you.

"Because it just is," you say.

You teach them other "glue words" for sticking two ideas together. They brighten every time they use one: *Studying is good* BUT! *it is hard. It is hard* YET! *it is fun.* You can suddenly imagine them sitting in Cambridge coffee shops wearing tight jeans and red shoes, absorbed by their own contradictions.

Some days you snap your ruler across your desk. "You must have *some* opinions. You must feel *one* way or another," you say, but they can't decide whether it is bad to drive drunk or good to wear sunscreen. They don't care about race relations or recycling, about the paparazzi or pesticide use. It is all good. It is all bad. It is all the same.

You go to Mr. Bruce.

"Too young for opyons. No such thing as opyon here," he says.

"That's ridiculous!" you argue. "An opyon is just a strong feeling. *Everyone* has strong feelings!"

He pulls a translation dictionary down from a high shelf, flips to the right page and passes it to you. Sure enough, the English entries leap from Opiate to Opossum.

"See?" he says, "No opyon here. Opyon is Amican."

You start to tell him that even if there isn't a word for it, the concept still exists, that even if the concept doesn't exist, it should, that opyons are a basic human right, but you notice he is staring at your mouth, looking so intently at it that his own mouth is twitching. You back out of the room.

AT HOME THAT night you write a letter to the people who designed the test.

To Whom It May Concern, you begin.

You cross that out.

Dear Sir or Madam, you begin again, *I am concerned that your test may favour students who share a specific set of—*A specific set of what? You can't seem to locate the phrase.

You tear that letter up, and the next and the next.

Dear Test Makers, you finally write, *My students sleep on dirt floors. They don't have shoes and have never heard of the British royal family. How do you propose I prepare them for Speech Topic #7 (Monarchies undermine democracy: agree or disagree)?*

While you are folding the letter, a mosquito—there are so many of them now—gets caught under your hand. It smears red and yellow across the page, limbs flattened out like a pressed flower. Beneath the mosquito you add: *P.S. For your information, some students don't have opyons on American problems. They actually don't.*

WITH THE TEST fast approaching, the other teachers start coming to work early and staying late, occasionally keeping students into the night. You suspect some teachers haven't been home in days. In his anxiety, Mr. Bruce has launched a school-improvement project. He has recruited some of the village men to add more tin signs to the outside of the building, and there is an endless stream of supplies flowing into the school basement, even after dark. The whole village seems agitated, aflutter. Inspired by all this industry, you begin to make detailed lesson plans for the rest of your stay.

Attendance starts to slip. Your students are needed at home. There are sick goats and dry wells and vegetable blights. They come and go as they please, but you decide not to involve Mr. Bruce. In the movies, attendance problems are a defining moment in any teacher's career. You've been expecting this, even hoping for it in a strange way.

IN THE END, you agree to the American names as a ploy to lure your students back. And how could you resist once they start pounding their desks, chanting "Amican names, Amican names, Amican names"? You have all the respect in the world for their given names and you really have tried to get those names straight, but their language has five tones, all in the nose. In class whenever you ask Pin Pon to stand, six of them rise. In the end, American names are just far more practical.

On the day you finally concede, you are writing a list on the board—Jennifer and John and Susan and Sean—and explaining that a name is a very personal thing when a fight breaks out among a group of girls who, apparently, all want to be called Madonna. It's the same thing on the boys' side of the room. Three of them who want to be called Rambo are jabbing each other with pencils. They are rabid, fierce. There are nosebleeds and splinters.

Once you finally calm them down, you manage to think of ten other timeless names and then hold a lottery. This is how your students come to be named Cyndi and Tiffany and Bono and Rocky. There is a Janet and a Michael, an Elvis and a Sinead, a Whitney and a Prince. The only one who doesn't participate in the lottery is the shy manure-smelling boy. He wants to be called Clong—the sound of a cowbell in the morning.

By the time the naming is settled, you can hear the other classes being let out. Mr. Bruce is pacing the hall. His shoes against the floor sound like *Harvard-Harvard-Harvard.*

YOUR STUDENTS GROW into their new names immediately. The girls start wearing their hair down. They stand a little taller and thrust their hips out when they walk. They wave to the boys using just their fingertips. And the boys have changed too. Even Rocky and Rambo are softer, more readable. During class you can see the emotions flicker across their faces—now lust, now boredom, now anger, now angst.

You begin to detect certain attendance patterns—the same boy-girl pairs absent on the same days. You try lecturing them on the importance of education above all else—even love. You remind them about Harvard, about the jobs they will one day get, the things they will be able to buy, but even the wildest shopping fantasies can't keep them all in the classroom.

THE AIR IS soupy with bugs now, and there is something else, a taste you can't quite place. Because it takes such effort to catch your breath, you wheel in Mr. Bruce's small TV and VCR. You will have your students watch key scenes from the medical drama they all love: the one where the young doctor gives a speech about losing her scholarship, the one where the paramedics debate resuscitating a pedophile, the one where the wife-doctor stands up to the mistress-doctor. Together you will draw a crude map of each scene on the board and then have them re-enact it. A multimedia classroom: your best idea yet!

MRS. ENGLISH TEACHER

When it comes time to map the scenes, you discover the subtitles they were reading told a much different story. In their scenes the young doctor was going off to war, the paramedics were faced with resuscitating an enemy soldier, the wife-doctor discovered her co-worker was an undercover spy.

You know you should lecture them about propaganda, about government censorship and subduing the masses, but you feel as if all the air has been punched out of you. Besides, they are excited, flushed, raring to go. You sit and watch as they run through the scenes without you. For the first time they are standing firm with an opinion: they *will* go off to war, they *will not* resuscitate the enemy, spies *should* be punished. Your more advanced students begin emoting. See how they bite their lips and run their hands through their hair? See how their chins tremble when they look off into the distance? They seem more American than ever.

At the end of class you gather them in a huddle.

"Now I understand," says Sinead. "Opyon is like acting!"

"It is like battle!" says Rocky.

"Like small war," says Rambo.

"Like pretend!" says Janet.

You think of certain nightspots and coffee shops at home and can't bring yourself to disagree with their findings.

"Congratulations," you say. "We really broke through today. Now we can move beyond small talk!"

"To what?" asks Clong. "Big talk?"

THAT EVENING, walking home under a lingering pink sunset, you vow to dive deep into Big Talk. You want to really find out who your students are, what they desire, what they're most afraid of. You will ask about their recurring dreams and then do fun partner-work involving Jungian analysis. You will get them to draw their feelings, to describe their families.

But in the morning when you get to school and write the word "fear" on the board, Rambo rises to speak on behalf of the boys. "We have no fear," he says and the rest of them bang their fists on their desks in a show of unity.

So they do have strong opinions!

"Excellent!" you say, crossing out "fear" and writing "war" above it. "What does war *mean* exactly?" you ask. "Why do some countries have wars and others not? What *exactly* is the purpose of a war? Is it *useful*? Is it *senseless* and *violent*?"

They can no longer follow. They are clamped down, their mouths pulled into mean little stitches, arms crossed tight over their chests. They have nothing more to say.

After a full hour of prickly silence, you come up with the mask experiment.

It seems like a great idea at first, but once the boys are lined up against the blackboard, wearing the girls' masks and looking at you with black seething eyes, once the very air has turned sour, you start to question the whole endeavour.

"Gender-role flexibility is the backbone of a healthy society!" you say, but you're only explaining your actions to yourself.

You had hoped for catharsis and group hugs and that certain kind of conversation that can only be compared to a river: rushing and fluid and of startling depth. You had hoped to crack them open.

"Ta-BOOH?" you ask. "Too much?"

Nobody laughs. The bell rings and they all file out. Many won't return.

THE AIR IS SWARMING, filled with flying ants, locusts and pale moths that move down the street like a fluttering fog. You have to duck into doorways while they pass. All those busy wings sound like sand poured from a great height.

When you ask him why all the bugs, Mr. Bruce says, "Refugees," but you can only assume he means migrants. Insect migrations: you saw a nature show on that once. Or maybe it's something more sinister. The air is so hot, so sweet and choking, perhaps someone is spraying pesticides in the next valley.

One day out of desperation, you tie a T-shirt over your nose and mouth to walk home. On the way, old men and women, the same ones you've passed every day since your arrival, look up from their chores for the first time. Their eyes lock onto yours, something like warmth passing between you. By the time you get home, you've cried clean trails across your cheeks. You find bugs pooled in your ears. You hadn't realized how invisible you've felt, how faceless and lonely. You quickly fashion your own mask from the sleeve of an old shirt. You will wear it everywhere but inside the classroom.

ONCE YOU START wearing the mask, and with just a month until the test, your students trickle back. The ones who have the farthest to walk stop going home between classes. At night they sleep huddled together at the bottom of the stairs. Many of their mothers have joined them there. After school, the women gather at the top of the stairs as usual, only now they are friendly. Now when you step over the threshold to go home, they come forward, clutching your arms and fingers. Their hands are cracked like leather. Their masks puff in and out with their chatter.

Whitney is the first to translate: "My mom wants to have you for dinner."

"Over for dinner?"

"Yes, over."

And so Whitney's mom is the first to pull you down the dusty road toward her home.

IN THE YARD, the men are sitting around a fire, telling jokes. They are spitting and polishing empty glass bottles.

"Not for Mrs. Teacher," Whitney says, leading you to the outdoor kitchen where you are introduced to the women and children. You help the children dish pickles and powders into an array of tiny bowls and then hand them off to Nug, a woman who looks about thirty, but acts about six. "Her brain never grew up," Whitney explains. Nug is the only woman not wearing a mask and she acts as a messenger between the men and women. Everywhere she goes her feet slap the ground, sending up dust clouds. Something about her broad, relentless smile makes you uneasy.

When it's time to eat, the men push a pile of branches aside to reveal a deep cooking hole. Fat sizzles off the rocks below as they hoist the meat up on long sticks. Nug squeals and claps her hands. For a moment, propped upright, the goat looks alive. It still has hide and bones, eyes and ears. It looks surprised, mid-stride, like it accidentally fell into a cooking hole.

When the men have finished serving themselves, Nug brings the remaining meat over to where the women are seated on the ground. You have already untied your mask and taken your first bite by the time you realize your mistake. Looking around, you see the other women have loosened the bottoms of their masks to create a kind of curtain. They smuggle their food up and under, up and under, like secret cargo. You quickly retie your mask, but you can feel the men looking at you across the distance.

AFTER DINNER, the men go back to their bottle-polishing and the women tuck in close. They are trying to tell you something, speaking softly, *shush, shush, shush.* Their hands are in your hair. The youngest ones cradle your curls delicately as if each one is a daisy chain. You feel protected, forgiven. And you feel something else too, an absence of desire, the sensation of being just exactly who and where you are.

You watch the men fill those bottles with a murky liquid. They are pushing rags into the bottles, sealing them off, and then Whitney's mom is next to you, reaching for your face.

"She wants a name, too," Whitney translates. "A Hollywood one."

You shake your palm in the air, the universal decline, but the women shake their palms back at you, mistaking it for a kind of wave.

"Please. It is great honour," Whitney says.

When you finally name her Farrah, Whitney's mom folds at the waist, weeping with joy. The women press against you, running their cold fingers up and down your arms. In a moment small hands are wiggling the earrings out of your ears. They are lifting the bracelets off your wrists, loosening the buckles on your sandals, tickling your skin. You catch a faint whiff of gasoline and your scalp hums. The women are all around you, shushing and clucking, *ooh*ing and *aah*ing. They are slipping your shoes off, sliding their own cracked and dusty feet over the smooth leather soles.

AFTER THE FIRST dinner invitation, the rest of the mothers want you to visit, too. They wait for you at the top of the stairs, arguing over whose turn it is. This is how you spend your last weeks. You eat, and then name your hostess Raquel or Loni or Olivia or Goldie. You give all of your belongings away and then float home barefoot under a blood-red sunset, wearing someone else's dress.

Lying in bed at night, smelling like meat and fire, you can barely remember how you used to fill your days at home. You try to picture your last apartment, but you can't even get as far as the four pastel walls. Was there a window? A door? In your mind's eye you try to picture yourself living that life, but the different parts of you—arms, legs, feet, head— always drift away from each other, like oil on water.

YOU ARE WALKING to school early on the Monday of your final week when you notice hundreds of footprints stretching out as far as you can see on either side of the road, as if every inch of ground has been danced upon. You are thinking about footprints, remembering your smart friend, when you notice thick grey columns rising up over the mountains. You are wondering if those columns are smoke or cloud and then something floats past your ear—a butterfly, not flying but falling sideways through the air to land softly at your feet. It's your first butterfly since you arrived in this country. You bend to get a closer look and see that it's burnt—its papery wings still smoking, its small black body crisp and hollow. You are just about to pick it up when another butterfly floats to the ground beside you, with one wing flaming blue. Soon they are landing—*pat, pat, pat*—all around. The sky is filled with them, burning butterflies tracing slow spirals through the air like maple keys. And then one is tilting toward you, still alive, burning and beating its wings. With each rush of air, the flames grow. Then, paralyzed, the butterfly coasts for a time, sinking lower and lower on shrinking wings. This struggle continues—the beating and the flaming, the coasting and the falling—until at last it hits dirt, wingless, with a body like a charred raisin. It is metamorphosis in reverse. And the smell is of burning shoes. And the silence is unbearable because this much death should make noise. In a moment it is you making the noise. You are shrieking, batting the air and running for the covered alley behind the market.

And that's when you see Nug, standing in the middle of the market, at the centre of a circle of men. You recognize some of them as the older brothers and young uncles of your students. Nug is looking up at the butterflies, hugging herself and whimpering, her face stretched into a silent scream. A butterfly flames past her nose and she wails and then the men close in on her. They push her back and forth, taunting, hissing, and their hands are all over her, on her breasts, her stomach, between her legs. They are raking at her clothes. Their fingers are on her face, in her mouth. And then her shirt is off and they are tossing it over her head, piggy-in-the-middle, and she is jumping, laughing with her sloppy, wide grin and the tears are fanning out across her cheeks. It is a game. She is laughing and crying, half-naked. And then they are pushing her to her knees, forcing her down.

You step out of the alley, screeching, throwing rocks, old fruit, whatever you can find. The men scatter. They slip away through cracks in the market walls and then it is just you and Nug and a thousand burning butterflies—the ground has grown soft with them. She is shirtless and shaking so hard her head looks loose on her neck. All around you the hills are burning.

AT SCHOOL, CLASSES have already started and Mr. Bruce is nowhere to be found. You get Nug settled in his office and then knock on Mrs. Diana's door.

"Mr. Bruce gone," she says.

"Gone where?" you demand. "What's going on here?" You don't mean to yell.

She peers over her shoulder at her class, then steps a little farther into the hall, closing the door behind. "Trouble coming," she says. "War coming."

MRS. ENGLISH TEACHER

You snort, more of a laugh really. You refuse to believe there could be a war approaching without your knowing anything about it!

But she doesn't laugh with you. Her eyes are deep and earnest, not black from this proximity but brown within brown within brown.

You can't, just now, remember home. You can't remember being anywhere but here, in this hallway, smelling of burnt wings, talking about war, as if it's a thing that can just sneak up on a person.

Down the hall, Nug is lolling on Mr. Bruce's desk, singing softly to herself.

THE FIRST THING you do when you step back into the classroom is make a big show of putting your mask on. The second thing you do is tell your female students to do the same. Then you instruct them to take out pencils and paper. Today they will be taking notes, you tell them, lots of notes.

You divide the board with two headings: *Good* and *Bad* and then you flip through the Speech book placing each topic on one side or the other. *Bad = Poverty, Oppression, Childhood Obesity, Poor Credit Rating, Discrimination, Weapons of Mass Destruction. Good = Democracy, Education, Retirement Savings Plans, Freedom of Speech, Sunscreen, Mammograms.* You dictate a short speech on each topic, going slowly, stopping often, so they can copy it all down. You will go through every topic this way. You will explain every last aspect of American life, telling them exactly what to think and why. You will keep them all night if you have to.

THAT NIGHT, WALKING home through the moonless dark, you can feel people running all around you, making footprints, getting ready. Fire glows in the distance. Butterflies caught in the updraft are shooting up over the hills, raining down like sparks on this side. It looks almost festive, almost like the Fourth of July.

IN THE MORNING, Mr. Bruce is back, sitting at a tilt on a bench in the school's entrance, drunk. When he sees you, he pats the bench beside him, "Seat, seat."

So you seat. You have so many questions and demands, but before you can get to them, while his eyes are still swimming slow circles around your face, he hands you a letter, already opened.

Dear Teacher,

Numerous focus groups and independent consumer trials have demonstrated the relevance of our test product cross-culturally. The most up-to-date research confirms...

You skip ahead.

... It is our understanding that the country you are stationed in is experiencing political upheaval. Studies have shown that our product may be less effective under such circumstance. May we suggest you visit the nearest American Embassy to ensure a safe passage home? Perhaps, once home, you would like to attend one of IELTA's many teacher-training seminars held bimonthly in key American cities.

You fold the letter and tuck it away. "So—war," you say. It isn't surprise you feel. It's a kind of relief, like being caught in the mouth of a hungry thing at last.

MRS. ENGLISH TEACHER

"Yuh, war," Mr. Bruce says.

"I'm not leaving," you declare. "I will not abandon my students. Not now."

"No X Test. No Ha-vad," he says. "Cancelled-cancelled."

"Can I still teach?" you ask.

"Yuh," he nods. "It can be so."

SO YOU TEACH even as your students disappear, one by one, boys and girls, to fight. You teach younger and younger students, first words, then phonics and eventually just the crude sounds of English. You teach because you can and because you've realized your mistakes, because you spent all that time on small talk when you should have been clearing the way to Big Talk, when you should have been talking to them about independence and freedom and the difference between right and wrong.

You continue to teach, even as the bullets ricochet off the school's tin armour, even after all the women and children are moved into the school basement, the room down there a cross between cellar and cave with its damp walls and its subterranean echo. When the pens and paper run out, you teach by grinding mosquitoes up into a paste to write on the cave walls. And when the mosquitoes run out, you scratch letters into the dirt. And then there is no need for writing anymore because the bodies have started to arrive—your students, returning to you again. Even those who are alive are changed, rearranged. Anything that was soft in them is now hard. Many are maimed and all of them have aged. Their eyes glint like hammered-down nails as they teach you, in perfect English, how to polish the bottle and soak the rag for a Molotov cocktail, how to stitch up a wound and set a bone. Patiently, they show you how to feel your way forward in a darkened cave and when to forget what you cannot save, and all the ways you do not belong to yourself.

the moustache
conspiracy

IT'S A BAD IDEA to paddle into the open ocean with Stefan as he is, Mary knows that. It's irresponsible, even reckless, but she's had it with resort life. That tiny cabin—so much wood, so little light, like living inside a walnut shell. The structured mealtimes—all those attempts to force friendship over slick buffet food. The whole place overrun with young hopeful moms in Lycra pants. Yes, she's had it with land, with people, with seasons and gravity, and the business of mothering, which is why she flirts with the man who's rented them the boats just long enough for Stefan to get a head start. Then she pushes off land herself. The man stands on shore, smiling and waving until he notices Stefan leaning dangerously in his kayak, looking like a rag doll stuffed into a toy boat. He walks briskly to the edge of the water and tries to call them back, but it's too late. They've almost disappeared into the bright white fog. Pretty soon the resort, the past, their entire landlubbing lives will shrink to a small dark embarrassment in the distance.

She saw the ad back in the spring. Stefan had been cooped up for months by then. *Adventure tourism* it said. Kayaks and canoes, fishing, a high-ropes course winding through old-growth treetops. *Old growth:* those words lit up in her mind. The website had shown groups of co-workers and juvenile delinquents dangling from harnesses in the cedar canopy, smiling despite themselves, as if all that looking down on the world had mended them. It wasn't long before her plan took shape. She put the house on the market, started whittling Stefan's pills with an x-acto knife and booked the cabin for the first two weeks of the off-season.

　Foolish to think a mother and her grown son could start again—she sees that now. But these past months, her hope got the best of her. As his pills shrunk week to week, he started walking and talking and asking for things again—apple juice, spaghetti, a new toothbrush—it didn't matter what. It had been so long since he'd wanted anything at all. She found a suitable buyer for the house. She even found doctors who agreed with her plans. "Yes!" her alternative psychotherapist, Dr. Bertrand, said. "Burn your old life maps!" Once Stefan was completely off his meds, he said they should both come back for a guided LSD trip. "Your spirit guides are very optimistic about this life change," said Lynne, her acupuncturist/psychic. Even her life coach agreed: The omens were good; it was time for action.

It wasn't until the drive up, though, that she realized how little he'd improved. He was lumped in the seat next to her and would speak only in single syllables, only in answer to her questions. Even then his voice was a growl, dredged up from some bottom she couldn't imagine. And there was a smell coming off him, like syrup or overripe fruit. She'd had to keep her window cracked open, enduring the screech of wind in her ear the whole drive. Beside her, he was busy keeping a tally, counting moustaches she guessed. There is something about men with moustaches. Not just that he doesn't trust them, but that moustaches are one of the ways the world is organized: some hierarchy or code—bushy versus thin, or dark versus light—she'd never understood it.

SHE WATCHES HIS boat lurch left-right, left-right with each dip of the paddle and wonders what she was really hoping to find out here on the water. Escape? Miracle? A beautiful end? He looks squeezed in, and she can hear him breathing through his nose like a fat man. She wonders if he can still swim, if he would even have the will, and then she holds her breath against this thought, waits for the one-two punch of grief-guilt—but it doesn't arrive. It seems the usual rules don't apply out here. After all, they're paddling into a fog so thick it's as if the sky has fallen. It parts in front of them and draws behind them like damp drapery. Out here everything is secret. Everything is forgiven.

WHEN THEY'D FIRST arrived, they were told the rest of the resort had been rented out for a "women's retreat." Those women were everywhere: in the dining room, in the kitchen, in the hallways, having such strange conversations, at such high volume.

"It's just—I feel as if my body is trying to tell me something," a woman at the other end of the picnic table said to her friend at dinner the first night.

"So dialogue with it," said the friend. "Say: 'Uterus, what *exactly* are you trying to tell me? I'm *just* not getting the message.'—Go on, try."

By the time Mary and Stefan had finished eating, the uterus had spoken and the woman had cried and her friend had suggested "supported headstands." Mary was wondering if this is what young women were really like nowadays or if this was just a troupe of actresses rehearsing when she noticed Stefan getting that look on his face—his eyes darting around the room, trying to take in all four corners at once like a trapped animal. She led him back to the cabin and opted to smuggle their dinners out of the dining hall from then on.

Stefan spent the first few days in bed, headphones on, sleeping or scribbling in his notebooks. She let him go, still hopeful, knowing he might feel worse before he felt better. He only got up to find food or use the bathroom. He'd return from the vending machines immediately, looking chased, with bags of chips and peanuts stuffed up under his shirt, but he'd stay in the bathroom for hours, doing who-knows-what with the door locked and the water running. That's when she picked up his headphones and discovered it wasn't music playing but static. She peeked in his notebooks and found page after page of strange math: *egg + house = home; family = momdad + dinnerguilt*. There were names of people they'd known, phone numbers, addresses, all laid out with lines and arrows between, as if to make a grand equation of their lives. She hoped for some wisdom or truth on those pages—*Home is where the egghouse is?*—but in the end they were incomprehensible. She closed the book. It was the engine room of a complicated mind—messy work best kept in the dark.

THEY PADDLE FOR an hour, two, straight into the fog and then pull close to pass a water bottle between them. "I'm big out here," Stefan mutters. They drift apart again. He's been talking more since they left the house. These days entire sentences float up, and every time parts of her float up too— ridiculous, stale-air parts. But he is still mostly incoherent, scrambled, as in a dream.

"He can't perceive his own borders," Dr. Wong told her once, just before he decided he would stop telling her these things. "He is everywhere at once."

"Foggy," Stefan says, passing the water bottle back to her.

"Yes," she says.

He is big and foggy. He is weather. He is wind. He is quantum, an exploded star, the pieces of him far and wide. This is how she's come to understand it. Understanding = making peace. Making peace = making pieces, swallowing, forgetting.

AT THE RESORT, Mary took long walks to get away from Stefan. It was a beautiful time of year, the last dry wheeze of summer, plus she enjoyed watching those women. She'd see them clutching their tummies and "visualizing abundance" in the forest, or lunging on the beach, stretching their abdomens, opening their fallopian tubes. It didn't take long to figure out this was some sort of fertility workshop, and then it became clear who was who. The fertile were grey and exhausted looking and talked the loudest. About home-schooling and goat's milk. About diapers, and how to save the world one person at a time. The infertile, meanwhile, were a little like babies themselves—wide-eyed and grabby—except they were always talking about their reproductive organs. No wonder Stefan was terrified.

After about a week she decided it was time to air Stefan out. She prodded him up from bed and out the door each evening during the dinner hour, when she knew the women would be sequestered in the dining hall. He snarled and resisted her at first, but once they made it past the resort grounds and into the safety of the forest he seemed soothed. Standing in the middle of a mossy clearing lit up by a low golden sun, he looked as if finally the world was right with him. Her hope ballooned. Maybe he could always be this satisfied, she thought, if the rest of life weren't so short on magic. Maybe this was progress, at last.

Then, on their way back from last night's walk, they rounded the corner of the dining hall and ran right into a gathering of women. They were kneeling in a circle, engaged in some form of toddler worship. At the centre of things, a child staggered after a dog, falling on it, trying to eat its tail while the kid's mother talked about hormone therapy, not to fear it, that it can produce a perfectly healthy child. The women were beaming after the child, and then all at once they aimed their smiles at Mary and Stefan.

Mary tried to say hello but Stefan bumped into her back and it came out short. "Hu—," she said. Stefan pressed his face into her hair, trying to hide behind her, the way he did as a child, only he was so much bigger than her now.

Just then the toddler bent to pick a stray cracker off the ground. He raised it to his mouth and, as if they shared a single paranoia, the women moved to intercept. "Don't!" the mother called them off. "I let him eat off the ground. It helps prevent—" she looked at Stefan and faltered—"illness down the road." The women settled again, a bunch of ruffled ducks, and their eyes floated back to Stefan and Mary. Stefan snickered from deep within Mary's hair and then, because laughter is contagious, because for a moment she saw the situation from the outside—an elephant-sized boy trying to wear his mother as a wig—Mary laughed too, an open-mouthed, rowdy laugh. The women looked at her with overblown horror, as if she were the spirit of infertility come to ridicule them, and then in another second she *was* the spirit of infertility and she *was* ridiculing them. *These women! Their crooked uteruses! All this planning, as if it will save their boys and girls!* She snorted and bent in half to contain herself. Stefan shuffled out from behind her then, exposed. Mary choked, felt her lungs fill with that particular kind of love that is inseparable from pity, inseparable from ache. It was too late to run. Those women stared.

If Mary was the spirit of infertility, then Stefan was a thing worse than that. He was fertility gone wrong, an unnatural thing all grown up. Mary tugged on Stefan's sleeve to lead him away, but he was watching the toddler and the dog share the soggy cracker—licking it, dropping it, licking it again. He was watching the women watching him. And then it was all too much. He clapped his hands to the sides of his head and let out a scream. It was monkey-high, pure animal. The dog barked. The women averted their eyes. Stefan ran and Mary followed.

HER SON IS a spectacle—no more getting around that fact. *If a spectacle kayaks off the map, is he still a spectacle?* she wonders and then realizes he's paddling so hard she can barely keep up. She calls out for a break, feeling like a child and an old lady at the same time. He senses what she's thinking, she reasons, and he's trying to get away from her. She thinks of that game they used to play when he was young, "What am I?" where one of them would think of something to be—a flower, a rock, an ocean—act it out and then get the other to guess. But after a while they were too quick for it to be any fun. "Dog!" Mary would shout before Stefan could get down on all fours, "sun" before his arms were halfway above his head. It became a kind of party trick, everyone convinced they'd rehearsed it.

Dr. Wong calls it their "capacity for sympathetic transfer." The people in her parent group call it codependency. The neighbours call it unhealthy. Everyone tries to frame it as his illness or her weakness, but Stefan and Mary have always lived this way, with their antennae out. She had tried to explain this to the doctors at intake but they weren't interested.

She had brought Stefan in because he was hiding in the basement for days at a time, because his life was more of a struggle than it needed to be, because the neighbours had found him standing in their gardens, listening to the flowers at odd hours of the night. Still, she had the feeling she could just as easily have decided not to bring him in. In those days she could still lure him upstairs with a grilled cheese sandwich. He would sit across from her, answering her questions, acting his old self for a time. It was on one of these days that he first tried to explain his moustache conspiracy to her—he was trying to warn her about the "new ironic moustache," that it was not at all what it seemed. He was panicked and ranting. She heard him out, but kept waiting for him to say he was just joking, it was all an act.

It was at intake that she met Dr. Wong. First came his questions—an interrogation that went on all night. She had the feeling she was betraying Stefan, helping the doctor catalogue his every oddity as the first signs of illness:

How he could suddenly be overcome with empathy for inanimate objects. That, on more than one occasion, he had run away with the ball in the middle of a soccer game because he couldn't bear to watch it be kicked anymore. Same with chess—he would get teary and start to protect the other pawns. She'd find them tucked into his bed days later.

His strange requests for Halloween costumes. A jellyfish one year. Forty-something rolls of Saran wrap. Another year, a doll's leg. Not the whole doll, just the leg. That, for several years, he slept with Band-Aids over his belly button, afraid his skin would come undone and slip off in his sleep.

That when his teachers wrote "So bright!" and "Imaginative!" on his report cards; they meant "bright" as in too much light, like a mirror stealing it from all around. They meant a Van Gogh imagination—the dangerous kind.

After hours of questioning, Dr. Wong finally made his judgment. "Schizophrenia," he announced. He was as grim as he was sure of himself. Schizophrenia: the too-tight sweater Stefan would have to wear the rest of his life. "Sorry," he whispered, and then he handed Mary a brochure for one of the parent support groups downstairs.

"THE DISEASE of too much imagination," one of the parents said at group the next evening.

"Too much plot," said another, and all the other parents nodded. Too many beautiful plots, that was exactly it. Trying to apply plot to a plotless world.

She made an appointment with Dr. Wong for the following morning to try that theory out on him. She wanted to confess how, during that golden stretch after she had gotten sober and before he hit puberty, she had probably spoiled Stefan a little, allowing him to sleep in her bed way past an appropriate age, reading as many stories as he wanted late into the night, even if it meant skipping school the next day.

"Is it possible he caught a bad case of the Grimms?" she asked. "You know, too many fairy tales too early? A set-up for failure?"

"Schizophrenia," he said. "Not your fault."

But all those magic beans and golden geese. The rest of the world such a disappointment. No wonder Stefan felt the need to story the gaps.

THE NEXT TIME Mary showed up for group, she wandered past her designated room. She couldn't see the benefit of sitting across from people just as stricken as her, and in all the same ways. Down the hall and around the corner she found another group about to start. It was for the parents of boys who'd become girls, girls who'd become boys, or those caught somewhere in the middle, a red-haired woman named Patty explained. Mary was informed that the ones caught in the middle wanted to be called "ze" instead of he or she, that it was the new pronoun of choice. "We have a joke," Patty said, "Jack and Jill went up the hill and came back Ze and Ze." Then she laughed too loud and for too long. Now this, Mary thought, is where she belonged. This was a celebration of parenthood, of imperfection, of children who had gone up the hill—over the hill—and come back changed.

Toward the end of the meeting, a man at the back rose to speak. He was wearing dirty pants, construction boots, an angry moustache. He was a newcomer, he said, and it was clear from the look on his face he wanted nothing to do with this brave new world of gender. He said his daughter had started with the hormone pills, that she now had tits *and* a beard, but he said it like, "Isn't it sick?"

"Tell you what, you take my boy to a game and I'll take your girl shoe shopping," Patty snapped. How she said it: "At least you still *have* a girl."

But the newcomer kept on about the "hormonal rains," about the fucked-up food chain. He was a monster, mad at the world. Still, some of what he said crept into Mary and stayed.

"JUST ONE MORE thing, Dr. Wong," Mary said at their third and final "outtake" appointment. "What about mercury poisoning?" He had the thinnest of moustaches, she noticed, barely there. Hard to trust a man like that. "What about the water, all those transsexual fishes and frogs?"

She told him about the strange dentist who'd done Stefan's fillings, how he'd flirted with her and then wouldn't take her money, about their neighbourhood, an estuary downhill from the city, a sponge for toxic runoff, all the other boys from their street queer or criminal or mentally ill, not one boy right, although the girls came out okay, got scholarships, moved away.

"No specific cause," Dr. Wong reassured her. He said something about predisposition, something else about this not being an appropriate venue for airing guilt.

But she wasn't done confessing. She was a mother onion rolling downhill, peeling herself as she went.

She told him about the time she'd found Stefan face down and bluing in the neighbour's pool; how, when her only job in the world was to count to five and blow, count to five and blow, her mind had spun out, unable to catch on the moment even as she felt him grow heavy against her lips. One whole minute before help arrived. How desperately she had loved him in that long minute. "What if I'd always been able to love him that much, Dr. Wong?" she asked. "What if I loved him that much now? Do you think it would bring him back?"

But Dr. Wong wasn't interested in love. He had made his diagnosis. Not even a drowning could throw him off course now. He wrote out a three-month prescription for Stefan, a psychiatric referral for Mary, and sent them both home. It wouldn't be the last time they saw each other though. It wouldn't be so easy.

THE MOUSTACHE CONSPIRACY

THEY'VE BEEN PADDLING for hours. The fog is lifting, brightening all around, but they are still heading toward a place they cannot see. She is dizzy—more than dizzy. She leans over the side of her boat to be sick but what comes up instead is an old prayer—*Take us, please.* Another heave, another prayer—*Take me instead*—and then she follows that thought down. Something else forming in the murky depths of her mind. A plea: *And if not me, then all of him, all at once.* She pictures him blue-lipped beneath her, remembers pushing the breath into his little body, like trying to force air into clay. Finally a kick deep inside his chest, a sudden opening through which he took everything—all the breath her body offered and then some. For the second time since his birth, she turned herself inside out, pushing life into him. For the second time, the great emptiness that followed. How easy it would be to knock him over now, she thinks, to hold him under with her paddle. How much better to move through grief, not to live there. And then, just as soon as she's formulated the thought, the fog slips past and the island they've been paddling toward hovers ahead like a mirage.

BACK ON LAND they slip into their usual roles. She sets up camp, and he sits in the sand, rocking back and forth, doing some sort of mental accounting.

"Firewood," she says, clapping her hands to startle him. As a boy, he'd spend entire days playing Can't Touch the Ground. He'd jump from rock to log, log to rock, collecting driftwood the whole length of the beach. Now he stands reluctantly and lumbers toward the treeline. He is as heavy-footed, as off-balance as a tourist.

She starts a small fire with what wood is lying around and then follows after him. The sun is setting now, everything sepia and shimmering as if she's moving through the memory of a forest. Every step sends up a fine golden dust. The smell of sweet, burnt vegetation, things crackling, coming apart underfoot. Then she sees him, standing off the trail in the thickest part of the forest. He is a statue of panic—a man realizing he has forgotten something—his wallet or passport—only what Stefan has forgotten is more essential: identity or purpose. He stands with his head tilted, listening to the air. She gets close enough to see he is trembling, muttering, and then he looks at her with eyes like emptied rooms. No sign of him there.

"Like he's possessed," neighbours used to say when they called to report he was standing in their back garden again. But by the time she could walk up the block to collect him, he'd always snapped out of it. This is the first time she's seen it for herself.

She steps closer and every part of him tenses. His arms lift ever so slightly as if he might swipe. His lip twitches into a sneer. Not her boy. Stefan has flown apart and in his place this animal, capable of anything.

"Okay, okay," she says and backs off, hands up, as if from an armed man. When she is finally out of sight she turns and runs. It is then, while running from Stefan—from her own boy—that she trips. She hits the ground nose-first, teeth-to-mud, like a human plow. Like a fool. The damage: fat lip, bruised chin, scraped knees and, above all else, blindness. Her glasses have flown off. She feels around in the blurry shadows, in wider and wider circles, trying not to cry. But the forest is cruel here. Trees crowd and whisper. Everything is menacing, is shuffling in the dark just out of sight. She can't make out the edges of things, keeps coming up on shapes sooner than she thinks, bumping into trees, roots, rocks, and then she can't find her way back to where she fell. Her glasses could be anywhere, in any direction. It is late, those long purple moments before full dark. She'll be lucky if she can find her way back to the beach.

No sign of Stefan when she comes crawling into camp. Just the embers of a fire left. She makes her way to where they dumped the camping gear and gropes around for food, the tarp, the knife. Boys, she thinks, they grow like weeds until the day they split open, the man in them pushing through. How sudden the change and how out of time—the urges of a man arriving before the intellect or morals of a man. The violence of a man. She grabs the sleeping bags but doesn't bother with the tent—they will sleep in the open air tonight.

AFTER DR. WONG sent Stefan home, the calls started. From the grocery store—he was burying notes in the bulk bins, kidney beans spilling out across the aisle. From the hardware store—he was tampering with the merchandise, writing messages on the backs of boxes. Soon he was banned from all the shops on the strip. She had to drive to faraway neighbourhoods to do her shopping. Her daily dilemmas narrowed to this: bring him along and risk embarrassment or leave him behind and risk his getting into trouble.

The medicine wasn't working, she told Dr. Wong. Where before his turmoil had been private, now it was worn on the outside, for all to see. "Isn't that worse?" she asked. "Aren't we aiming for better here?"

What Stefan most likely needed was more, Dr. Wong said and increased the dosage.

Stefan became jittery and stopped sleeping. He was on alert, hyper aware of whatever was coming next. He would jump just before the doorbell or the phone. He developed a new maniacal laugh, then a fear of blinking, then a habit of standing bug-eyed in the corners of rooms, watching everything. He became non-verbal but not for lack of things to say. She could still see movement, the tail-flick of intelligence, in the darks of his eyes.

Dr. Wong increased the dosage again. It seemed he was rooting for the medicine more than for Stefan. Then the business with the moustaches escalated. He started pacing the sidewalks, yelling at every moustache that passed by. He would follow some moustaches halfway across town, others he would duck into bushes to avoid. He started breaking into people's houses, drawing moustache hieroglyphs on the walls. There were teams as far as Mary could tell—good versus evil—and he was some sort of spy. He was ze, caught in the middle.

Then one day the unthinkable.

She unrolls their sleeping bags on opposite sides of the fire. The terrible things that happen by the sides of highways, in basements, under bridges. That farmer who killed all those hookers and fed their bodies to his pigs. That student who dismembered and barbecued his ex-girlfriend. All those men who were boys once. All their mothers, with no idea. She zips herself in, relieved he's not back yet, and then afraid of what he might do, and then asleep, with the knife clutched to her side.

SHE WAKES and for a long moment can't remember who she is. Then she can remember who but not where. Then she can't remember how to operate her mouth. She sits up, choking. A faint glow in the distance—*Stefan's night light?* She must be in the upstairs hallway, except the light is jittering. She must be drunk. Then water sounds, wind, and memory starts to trickle back. She remembers kayaking, Stefan standing in the woods, losing her glasses. She remembers that there is no house anymore, that this is their new start, their last chance, their beautiful end. She looks around but the night is an indecipherable smudge. She gets on her hands and knees and feels her way to the other side of the fire.

"Stefan?" She reaches for the edge of his sleeping bag but he's not there. "Stefan?"

Nothing.

Water sounds and that strange light growing larger in the distance as if it's bearing down on her.

"Stefan!" She can't hear herself over the waves.

Still nothing.

Her heart flutters, triple beats, then a long desperate syllable, "Maaaa," from behind. She crawls back toward him. He must've moved his sleeping bag next to hers in the night. His hand finds hers in the dark and the world rearranges itself again, everything in its place. Water ahead, sky above. And that light across the water must be the resort, lit up like a dancer in bright skirts.

"The house is burning down," he says.

The size of the fire has quickly doubled—a chorus line of dancers now, the whole resort surrendering upwards.

She wonders for a moment if it was her, if she forgot to turn something on or off, but before she can rule herself out Stefan looks at her, fully present for the first time in months, and says, "I did it." There are two small fires in his eyes. He is wide open, terrified. It's a look she's seen before—that day she pulled into the driveway to find a crowd of hissing neighbours, an angry father, a ruined mother.

The neighbours were ferocious, pounding at her windows. When she stepped out of the car, they swarmed, yelling on top of one another: *Stefan's got our girl!—Jumped out of a bush and ran off with her!—Holding her hostage in the basement, fucking pervert maniac, doing who knows what!—Police on their way!—Open the fucking door!*

She didn't open the door. She hurried around back and locked herself in.

She may never understand what she found that day. Chelsea, tipped over on the ground, babbling softly, her wheelchair upended. Mary's first thought: Of course it's the disabled girl, something familiar about this scenario. Her second thought: At least she won't tell. Chelsea with a thick black moustache drawn on her upper lip, sucking her fingers, seemingly content except she was sitting in her own puddle. Her pants undone, a clean towel folded on the ground next to her. Had he tried to change her, or was this something much worse? On the other side of her a plastic bowl of water, duct tape, a pen and flashlight. Was this violence? Stefan came rushing into the room then, a roll of toilet paper in his hands. Without even acknowledging Mary, he unspooled it to sop up the mess. Wet piles everywhere. Was this kindness?

They moved quickly then—accomplices. "We're okay," Mary kept saying. She found sweatpants—*We're okay*—changed Chelsea, sat her back in her chair—*We're okay, we're okay*—fixed her ponytail, even gave her a juice box before they heard the sirens. Then she gave Stefan all the money she had in her wallet and helped him sneak out the bathroom window. What had she envisioned for him? A glorious getaway? A life on the lam? Monthly postcards from deepest Mexico?

He made it halfway down the block before they caught up. It took eight men to bring him down. A dog pile of cops and neighbours. Stefan at the bottom, shrieking and laughing in sock feet, his blue-black moustache smudged.

He was committed. Not exactly schizophrenia, the doctors said this time, although closely related. Not quite a mood disorder, although Stefan's moods were certainly disordered. Not quite autism, but not unlike it in presentation. Not quite psychosis, although he would need to take antipsychotics for the rest of his life. Not brain injury *per se,* although areas of the brain were affected. They ran tests and tinkered with his medicine for weeks—medicine chasing the side effects of medicine in a great loop. By the time she was finally allowed to visit, what he resembled most was a zoo animal, caged and asleep in the back corner of himself.

At the hearing they read aloud the things Mary had said at Stefan's intake. Dr. Wong was there to comment on Mary's suitability as a caretaker. They read the police report, letters from neighbours, and then they sent Mary and Stefan home under strict probation: he would take his meds and attend outpatient therapy, she would begin therapy herself and attend a three-month "caregiver workgroup." It felt like divorce—a combination of private fear and public shame. She had shared too much and now she was being punished. Now she had to take this strange man home, this whale of a man who had swallowed her son whole, and learn how to love him. It was humiliating. It was tits and a beard—more than she could bear.

Now this. Arson. Possibly murder. She thinks of all those someday mothers back at the resort, of the staff, of the man who rented them the boat—all barbecued now. And here she is, just one more stupid fool who thought, *Not my boy,* right up until the last minute.

"My fire," Stefan says and he is up, heading for his kayak. It's only once he's walked away that she remembers that doctor—not even a doctor, a male nurse—who had stopped her in the hospital lobby about a week after Stefan had been admitted. "I know your boy," he'd said. Mary had started to back away, but he wouldn't let her go. He held her by the wrist and did what no other doctor or nurse has since. He asked how she was taking it all, if there was anything she needed. He spoke to her like an old friend, like it was her turn to talk, he would wait.

"I just wish I knew what he's feeling," she finally said. "I want to understand."

His answer: "Imagine your guilt is a city and you are lost in it. Everywhere you go, every bad thing you see, it's all your fault and you can't find your way home." He flung his arm to take in the room, the city outside the hospital doors. "Imagine feeling responsible for all of this, all the time."

It's only once she remembers Stefan's city of guilt, his sprawling sense of responsibility, that she realizes he didn't start the fire, couldn't have. She stumbles down the beach after him, but by the time she can catch up he has already pushed off into the night, into the water whose features she cannot read. Forever his accomplice, she gets into her boat and follows.

SHE REMEMBERS the sea as a landscape—mountains piggybacking mountains, valleys steep and narrow. She remembers how the wind ripped the paddle from her hands and set her spinning like a toothpick in a drain, then tipping into the cold water and her limbs struck dumb. *If we get out of this.* She doesn't remember a thing after that, until she was hauled up into the light.

Now she is blanketed, with a cup of something so hot it feels cold. Her vision is blurred but she can see she's on a boat within boats, that they're all tied together and people are climbing up from the different holes. She keeps trying to put her cup down and stand, but every time a man with an eye patch pushes her down, puts the cup back in her hands. *Drink,* he says. *Keep warm.*

She looks around, takes in all the hats and patches and hooks and headscarves and understands—they've been rescued by pirates. Her stomach curls up, dies a little. They're holding Stefan captive somewhere, or worse. She thinks of the terrible things that must happen on high seas—drunken rituals, human sacrifice.

The pirates keep asking her the same questions—her name, the date, where, why, over and over—but she can't answer. In the distance she hears people screaming, the wet thud of bodies hitting water. *The plank,* she thinks, and then she calls out for Stefan.

They crowd around, talking about her as if she's not there. Soon they'll ask for her wallet. After that, who knows? *Cubbyshock, cubbyshock,* they keep saying. She doesn't trust her ears. Everything is stuttering. She closes her eyes tight and when she opens them again, Stefan is beside her. *Could be shock. Give her some space.* He hugs her, holds her hand. He is smiling—she doesn't understand why he's smiling—and his skin and hair are sparkling, greenish-white. *We're okay, Mom. You're in shock, but we're okay.*

The pirate approaches with another hot drink. She jumps. Stefan understands then: it's that old game, "What am I?" She is Fear.

It's just costumes, he says. *Halloween early, for the kids.* She looks around then and sees not just pirates, but mermaids, cats, bearded ladies. Children too—little ghosts, mice, princesses. And strange gourds carved into jack-o'-lanterns.

Sails up and not for sailing. Just because. Lights, music. A bunch of hippies having a party. Not pirates.

The man who brought the drink lifts his eye patch—two kind blue eyes—and sits next to Stefan. Soon they are talking about solar heating, and vegetable gardens. Other people join in. *Off-grid,* the pirate keeps saying. They live out here, off-grid, all year round. They go to shore a few times a year to get everything they need. Some people have cabins tucked away on these small islands, some have gardens or greenhouses.

A few of us haven't stepped on land since the Vietnam War, the pirate says proudly.

Can't touch the ground, Stefan says.

Exactly. The pirate laughs. Everyone laughs. *That's exactly what!*

Then it's Stefan's turn. He talks about life on land, about Walmart, Starbucks, the cops, then he starts in on his usual rant: *Ever notice how moustaches aren't the same as they used to be? Used to be you could tell what kind of man, but now...*

Everything in Mary pauses. This could be it, Stefan's moment of spectacle.

On one of the other boats a piñata bursts. Hard candy rain.

She pulls on Stefan's sleeve to lead him away—if there was a plank she would walk it—but she has no strength.

Yeah! Yeah, I did notice that, the pirate answers. *I keep seeing all these young guys with these old-guy moustaches.* He pats Stefan on the back and cackles. *That's right!*

Someone else joins in. *I got one. Ever notice how dogs aren't how they used to be? I mean, who's really in control, the dogs or the owners?*

And another: *Did you hear the* CIA *invented Facebook to keep track of everyone after 9/11?*

They circle around, talking about radio waves and cities and government surveillance. Stefan has popped the lid on something, given them all permission to vent. He stands at the centre of it all, looking proud and perfectly at home here, among these pirates and mermaids and conspiracy theorists.

She drops her hand from his sleeve and notices her own skin sparkling blue-green. She wants to ask someone about it but she's tongue-tied, too tired to find the words. Then it occurs to her, maybe no one else can see these sparkles, maybe they've been secretly winking out at her these past months, her own private Morse code, showing her the way.

The pirate sees her looking and leans in. *Phosphorescence,* he says. And when that doesn't register: *Organisms in the water. Amazing little guys. They collect sunlight all day long and glow all night.* He leans over the edge of the boat and scoops up some water. *See.* The water flashes in his hands, shy glitter.

On the next boat, kids are suddenly tearing off their costumes. They can't get them off fast enough. Everyone stands to watch as the kids jump into the water—one-two-three-four—all on top of each other. An explosion of neon light where they land, a solar system of bright bubbles rising all around them.

Mary shivers. It wasn't long ago she was gulping that water.

They'll be all right, the pirate says at her side. *There's a warm current here, comes all the way from Japan. The only reason you two are still alive.*

The kids are putting on a show now. They look like electric frogs with their arms and legs lit up green. Even the water running down their hair and into their eyes is glowing.

Stefan laughs loud with his mouth hanging open, eyes flashing in amazement. It's a look she hasn't seen in years. Finally the world was behaving as it should. Glow-in-the-dark water. Tropical currents. Here at last was a little bit of magic.

She sits down, closes her eyes, and next thing the pirate is carrying her down into the belly of the boat. Someone is playing a mandolin in the corner. The place smells of chili and cornbread. She is tucked into a narrow bed and the people are bringing blankets, hot water bottles. Above her, a homemade mobile turns slowly—beach glass, feathers, driftwood, bones. Something about that mobile tells her that risking everything these past months was worth it. The omens were good. A million secret little lights were leading her all along, to this.

Just before she drifts off she remembers the bargain she made, out there in the water, her final offer to a disease that has never played by the rules. *If we make it through this, I'll be the sick one.* Now, lying in this soft pirate's bed, mute and strange even to herself, she knows the bargain has been accepted. And she knows that tomorrow she will go back on land long enough to buy the first sailboat she sees. Then she'll sail out here and tie on with the rest of the pirates. Yes, tomorrow it begins: Can't Touch the Ground for as long as it will last.

drift

THE LAST TIME Lena's mother calls, everything seems normal. Normalish. Normal enough.

Lena is standing in the Shark Museum at the time, looking into the mouth of a huge taxidermy shark. Mr. Kapp, the proprietor, lost his arm to this very shark decades ago, but now, it seems, they cohabit peacefully. The shark's head takes up most of the living room but acts as a kind of coffee table.

"And where do you call from now?" Ama yells in her thick Slavic accent. Already she forgets she's the one who dialled.

"New Brunswick," Lena answers. Best to leave the shark out of it. It's the little things that confuse Ama these days.

"New Bruns-*who*?" Ama shouts. This isn't forgetfulness, Lena reminds herself, but Ama's brand of humour. All across Canada it's been the same: Mani-*who*-ba, On-*who*-io, *Who*-bec. She waits a beat and sure enough Ama gives her signature "Ha!" to indicate she's joking. "And how is the museum?" she asks next.

Lately, Ama seems to have forgotten Lena promotes museums in general, rather than working at, say, the gift shop of one in particular. Lena doesn't correct her. She's decided not to give too much negative attention to these little slip-ups. Besides, her career has recently tanked and she doesn't want to get into it.

"It's fine," she says, following a group of adults into Mr. Kapp's dining room. Looking at the hole Mr. Kapp cut into the wall to make way for the shark's midsection, seeing how the drywall is shredded, not unlike a shark bite, a small sadness blooms in her stomach. This is the kind of thing she would have been able to share with Ama once. Once they would have laughed about it, but now it would just disorient her.

"Your brother, Yakov, likes old things too," Ama says in a faraway voice.

Lena pauses. She doesn't have a brother or know anyone named Yakov.

People back home have warned her this might happen. They say Ama has been calling everyone old-world names lately and asking them to fetch water from the well, but Lena is pretty sure most people just don't get Ama's humour.

"Funny!" Lena says, laughing loud, "but, seriously, how is the fortune-telling?" Ama has been reading palms out of her home since Lena was young.

"Is fine," Ama says, snapping back to the moment. "So tell me, how you find husband when always you are running? Why you don't come home and have me my grandkids?" Lena can feel her heart beating in her ears. Before the abortion, this used to be Ama's rally cry—"Come home, find man, make baby"—but it's been years since she's heard it. She never told Ama what she'd done, of course, but she always suspected Ama knew.

At this point in the conversation Lena would usually change the subject, reminding Ama that she is the "Museum Lady," that one-point-five museums close their doors every week, and if she isn't travelling the country documenting their collections, all that history will be scattered in junk shops across the nation. But it's been a bizarre week. On Monday—the high point of her career—she received the news that she had been declared a "Great Canadian" by the Heritage Canada Foundation. Then, on Friday—the end of her career—she found out her Canada Council for the Arts funding has been cut and her publisher isn't interested in any more museum books.

Lena wants to say "There is no more 'Museum Lady.'" She wants to tell Ama the story of her week, to confess about the abortion and explain that it just wasn't the right time, but it would only overwhelm her. "Someday, Ama," she says instead, "maybe someday." She's distracted. Some of the adults have recognized her from a spot she did on the local news several weeks back. Plus, Ama is having one of her coughing fits. It sounds tubercular, like empty boxes falling down a flight of stairs.

Looking for the nearest exit, Lena notices another ragged hole cut into the back of the house where the shark's tail continues into the yard. She slips out the back door just in time to spot a teenager carving his initials into the tail fin with a Bic pen. "Hey," she shouts, marching over to grab the pen out of his hand. She says a hurried goodbye to Ama, promising to call next Sunday, gives the kid a short lecture on the sanctity of historical artifacts—even shark tails—and then—purely for showmanship—snaps the pen in half.

BACK IN HER CAR, wiping ink and plastic splinters off her hands, Lena is willing to admit she's been feeling a little out of sorts.

"You're grieving," her friends say. "Your mom has dementia, possibly Alzheimer's. It's normal to be sad."

Dementia, Alzheimer's, grief: lately people have been dropping these words like casual bombs on her life.

"This isn't about Ama," Lena insists. "Ama is fine."

Lena knows Ama is less than sharp these days, but then she always was a little too sharp. She's probably just mellowing in her old age. The neighbours say Ama's grasp on the present has grown slippery, that each time she goes for a long walk in her nightgown, a little less of her comes back, but Lena still doesn't see any reason for alarm. Ama can be a little vague from time to time, but she can also be perfectly lucid. Perfectly charming. Perfectly herself.

"Ama is a psychic and a refugee," she tells her friends. "She's spent her whole life ignoring the past or lost in the future. No wonder she gets confused!"

"Mmmhmm," her friends say. "Denial. It's part of the grieving process."

Lena hasn't been herself lately, it's true. Yes, she's been making eyes at men in bars, in cars, in her rearview mirror during rush hour. True, she's been following her GPS to pubs in the middle of the day where she drinks too much and accidentally dances into the arms of strangers. And, yes, she did wake up in her car one morning this week, wearing men's socks, with matted hair and metallic breath, something like chicken bones sucked clean at her feet, and no memory whatsoever of how she got there. But she wouldn't call it grief exactly. More like spiritual vertigo. More like the soul's black ice, the long, drawn out skid before the crash.

THE CRASH COMES later that same week when Ama's neighbour, Mrs. Winnow, calls to say Ama is gone.

Lena is standing in Burt's Burl Museum at the time, surrounded by burl clocks, burl ashtrays, burl tables and chairs. Burt recently succumbed to a rare disease in which he was overtaken by burl-like tumours, inside and out, so his widow, Sandy, has been giving Lena the tour.

Lena gestures that she has to take the call and ducks out of the room. "What do you mean, *gone?*" she says. "Gone where?"

"Missing," Mrs. Winnow says, sounding guilty. She's the one who assured Lena the neighbours would keep an eye on Ama until Lena could return.

"Did you check the grocery store?" Lena asks. "And the mall?" She now stands before a memorial wall documenting Burt's struggle with his disease. It seems he was in and out of hospital for years, having one tumour after another removed.

"Well, that's the thing," Mrs. Winnow says. "It's been a couple of days."

"A couple of *days*!" Lena has become a louder, more startled echo. "It's winter! She could be frozen in a ditch somewhere! Did you call the hospitals, the homeless shelters?"

"We've checked everywhere," Mrs. Winnow says, "absolutely everywhere. It's like she's vanished into thin air."

"Vanished? Into thin air? That's your best guess?" But looking at the pictures of Burt in various hospital beds, hooked up to various tubes, she wonders if vanishing isn't the better option.

Mrs. Winnow explains that Ama has been acting funny lately, that she's been running errands and talking about going back to the old country.

Lena starts to hyperventilate. Ama doesn't run errands. In the past thirty years she's barely left the house.

Mrs. Winnow goes on to explain that Ama left a note.

"What does it say?" Lena asks.

"'Gone home.'"

"That's all?"

"And 'Love, Ama.' It says that, too."

Lena leans against the wall to steady herself. "So what are you saying?"

"I'm saying, do you think it's possible she went back?"

"No," Lena snaps, "there is no *back*." These are Ama's words, not her own. Words she's heard all her life, along with "Past is past" and "Never mind before."

"Ama would *never* go back," Lena reiterates. "Let's just keep looking for her here, in *this* country. I'm on my way home."

LENA DRIVES THROUGH the night listening to a tribute show for a maritime folk legend on the CBC. Normally she wouldn't tolerate this sort of thing but she's trying to behave like a Great Canadian. Plus, all these ballads about lonely lighthouses and widows left ashore seem appropriate somehow. She too feels shipwrecked and motherless. Come to think of it, she feels downright seasick—nauseous and woozy in the knees.

Interspersed with the songs are interviews. *Oh, but he sure did know a song for every occasion,* the man's friends say. They sound almost Irish with their swollen vowels and pointy Ts. *Oh, but there wasn't time to write 'em all down, he was gone so fast.*

This idea of missed moments and lost songs seems to Lena like the saddest thing in the world and soon she is having one of those good, hearty CBC cries—the kind of cry that doesn't really count because it's wholesome and patriotic, and besides she's in her car where no one can see. She changes the station again and then again, but because of Canadian Content Rules, it seems they're all playing Neil Young at this late hour: sad songs about Northern Ontario, about low moons and the endless search for a heart of gold. She knows it's dangerous to think about one's mother while driving down the highway listening to Neil Young, so she snaps the radio off. But in that special silence that comes after Neil Young, she can't stop thinking that she too has lived her whole life in pursuit—not of golden hearts, but of the old country, her own lost song.

Lena has only ever been able to remember the past as a kind of fever dream—a smear of heat and colour at the outer edges of thought. She knows they escaped a war and were chased through the mountains. She remembers trudging through the night and fear as a feeling in the knees, but as soon as she tries to latch onto facts—who was chasing them and why—her memory yawns, dark and wide.

Lena longed for the old country the way any child would long for something half remembered. She spent years begging Ama to talk about it, but there was only one story she was ever willing to share. Even then, it wasn't really intended for Lena, but was a kind of performance piece Ama liked to put on for her Canadian friends.

"My Lena was born in a cave, in mountains, in middle of war," Ama would begin.

Lena was born fist-first and all at once, the story went, and when she landed on the cave floor she opened her eyes and smiled. The women in the cave crowded around, declaring her a "perfect April potato," which in that part of the world was the highest compliment for both people and potatoes. But then, a moment later, Lena roared and the women had to reinterpret the signs.

"Two things they saw," Ama would say, holding up her fingers for effect. "One: she would be stubborn, always. And two: we would live through war." Here her friends would nod—*Yes, yes, Lena the stubborn. Lena the potato.*

"She was perfect war baby," Ama would continue, "but heavy like bowling ball." According to the story, she'd had to venture down into the nearest town to get a special carrier made by a man who normally made horse saddles. She'd had to give two eggs, a lump of bread and her last scrap of decency for that carrier but it was worth it because it meant she could walk through the night with Lena sleeping on her back.

"We walked straight out of war," Ama would finish up cheerfully, "and into brand new life."

At this point whoever Ama was telling the story to would sigh and fold their hands in their lap. Canadians loved stories of distant wars and narrow escapes. But Lena was never satisfied.

"You missed the best part," she would interrupt. "How long did we walk for? And to where? And *why* was I so heavy?" She imagined the worst—milk heavy with mercury, shrapnel-laden potatoes, herself as an infant teething on rocks.

"Stubborn, no?" Ama would say to her friends and then they'd laugh and move off to another part of the house.

CROSSING INTO QUEBEC at dawn, Lena feels queasy and hungry at once. Is this grief, she wonders, or denial? Her tires *tha-wump, tha-wump* over the rutted highway. Good old Quebec, she thinks, Canada's collective dream of another time and place. Here was a part of Canada that longed for the old world, a place that didn't fix its roads and wasn't afraid to look back. The province's motto, *Je me souviens*, stares out at her from every licence plate. It occurs to her that Quebec is the mother she always wanted: one foot in the future, one foot in the past. Not like Ama. If Ama had a motto it would be *Forget, Forget, Forget*.

Old world, new world: it was a constant source of tension between Lena and Ama. As a kid, when Lena brought home war documentaries and maps of Eastern Europe, when she asked where they were from and why they had left and who they had left behind, Ama would say, "Never mind old country." She would clench her fists and turn red in the face. Then, like a switch being flipped, she would glom onto the future. "Tell me, when is senior prom?" she would say, brightly. "What will you wear?"

"This is Canada," Lena would explain. "We don't do prom here."

"But how do the girls meet the boys?" Ama would ask. "You must have Canadian cheerleading? You must have Canadian frat party?" Everything Ama knew about Canadian life, she'd learned from American TV.

Lena was never Canadian *or* American enough for Ama. In grade school, Ama started pressuring her to hang out with the Jennifers and Susans and Christines from her class, but Lena refused. She always felt on the wrong side of something vast and whooshing around these girls, something she couldn't quite place: History? Mystery? Pain?

She dressed like an immigrant and had dinner-smelling clothes. They had sisters and fathers, pierced ears, pink bedrooms.

She liked world news and war documentaries. They liked boys.

She had a heavyweight past full of shrapnel and vague trauma. They were jazz dancers and gymnasts, bird-boned, with hearts like kites.

By high school it was all-out war. "How you find Canadian boyfriend looking like that?" Ama would say over breakfast. Then she would stand guard at the front door shouting, "More makeup!" and "Stuff bra!" and "Make bigger your hair!" When Ama started reading the fortunes of all the popular girls from Lena's school, Lena took an after-school job at the local museum. When Ama refused to speak the old language, Lena refused to speak English. When Ama dressed like a teenager, wearing dangly earrings and shiny shirts, Lena dressed like Ama, wearing her old skirts and clogs. They moved through the apartment in icy silence. That is, until the day Lena decided to follow Ama room to room, singing questions about her father to the tune of "Frère Jacques." That was when Ama finally decided she'd had enough. She turned on Lena and smacked her halfway across the room, hissing, "Past is past," in such a way that Lena finally got the message: with Ama the past was—would always be—off limits.

For two years after Lena moved away to university she avoided Ama's calls. It wasn't until her third year, when she started volunteering at a refugee centre and met so many others who were desperate to forget the past that she started speaking to Ama again. But by then Ama had grown soft and confused, occasionally mistaking Lena for her clients or for television characters. By then it was too late.

Lena bites her lip, turns the radio on and up. It's Canadian Content again: Neil singing: "Old man look at my life..." She turns it off.

No, she thinks, looking out at all the marshmallowy drifts of snow lit up pink and gold in the morning light, there is absolutely no way Ama—or anyone in her position—would go back. It's a code among refugees: no back, only forward.

She spends a few minutes trying to think of all the friendly places Ama might have wandered off to—a spa? the circus? The bedding department at the Bay?—then calls Mrs. Winnow to explain the code of refugees, and to make a few suggestions about where else she might look.

LENA IS SOMEWHERE outside of Montreal, sitting at a diner known for its upside-down hamburgers when she gets the call.

"And where are you now?" Ama starts.

Lena is so excited she nearly drops the phone. "Montreal," she says. She is about to describe the concept of the upside-down burger, when she catches herself. She should be hurling questions, demanding answers. No, she should be soft. No, firm.

"*No*, Ama," she says, settling on stern. "Where are *you*?" She is yelling, just a little.

"Djurdjevik," Ama says. "Can you believe?" The line is full of loud air, as if she's calling from a distant planet.

"Durda-*what*?" Lena searches her purse for a pen, then stops. "What is that, a mall? How do you spell that?"

"Is hot here," Ama says. She is giddy, like a little girl using a tin-can phone. "And my old friends are here."

"You must be mistaken, Ama," Lena says. "Are you inside? Are you at a rec centre or a bus station? Tell me what you see."

"I see chickens," Ama says. "And donkeys. I see the woman setting up for market and the old man spitting—"

Everyone must be right about the dementia, Lena thinks. Ama must be in a mall. She must be seeing reindeer and Santa and his elves.

"No, Ama," Lena interrupts, speaking in a tone usually reserved for toddlers and bad puppies. "None of that's real. Now, I need you to focus and tell me where you are."

A long echoey silence in which Lena tries to decipher the background noises on Ama's end of the line. She hears what could be a rooster, or a cell phone, what could be a cowbell

DRIFT

or an ATM machine, distant music or possibly muzak. Then, much closer, a soft pop like a dropped egg—something fragile burst open—and, for the first time Lena can remember, Ama is speaking the old language. Suddenly she is eloquent, and Lena is struggling to keep up.

In a low, bluesy growl Ama starts to tell a story of a day, long ago, when soldiers were spotted coming down the village road, how the women had to rush around hiding the children up trees and under beds and in the chicken coop.

Lena is briefly elated until she remembers this is no time for stories, even if she has waited her whole life. "Ama," she interrupts, "do you see that friendly man with the red suit and the white beard? Can you hand him the phone?" But Ama pushes on. When the soldiers got to town, she says, they gathered all the women, tied them to the trees and shot their guns until, one by one, the children emerged.

Lena feels an old familiar fluttering in the knees—fear, alive in the body. "What did they do with them?" she asks. The question flies from her mouth, a bat from a cave.

Another long pause. Ama says something about running in circles, about guns and dust, but in the middle she breaks into a rumbling cough. Something swells in Lena—a memory of how, those first weeks in Canada, Ama would curl up with her at night, whispering fairy tales. There was one about a woman who waited so long for her husband to come back from the war, she turned to stone—or was it a statue? And there was another about children—a whole village of them—who vanished one day in a puff of smoke.

"The children. All dead," Ama says, still wheezy from coughing.

"And the women?" Lena asks. Another dark, flying question.

They were tied to the trees for days, Ama says. And then, finally, the men made them crawl back to their houses on all fours, with ropes around their necks.

"Like dogs," Ama says, switching to English and then the line breaks up and dies.

Lena closes her phone, looks down at her upside-down burger, which must have arrived at some point during the conversation and is, it turns out, just a regular burger with the top and bottom buns reversed. Whatever swelled in her a moment ago now bursts. She turns quickly and vomits into her purse.

LENA DRIVES INTO Ontario searching her memory for the day Ama spoke of, but it's no use. She remembers the long walks at night, huddling around low fires, hiding beneath Ama's skirts, but no soldiers, no guns. She searches her soul for a village of ghosts, but comes up empty. Not one.

Still, she must've been in the village that day, she thinks. Why else would Ama tell the story now? Why else would her body feel like wet concrete, her skin like rubber, her joints like they've made a secret deal with old age? Her body must know what her mind can't comprehend. Maybe she hid under the floorboards the way children are always doing in the movies. Maybe she and Ama were the only two to escape and that's why Ama never wanted to talk about it. Maybe she really did eat shrapnel-laden potatoes.

She thinks of the village from Ama's story and wonders what happened to the women once they were taken back to their houses. Then all the small hairs of her arms stand at attention as she recalls another fairy tale Ama told about a village of women who turned into a pack of rabid dogs overnight.

She switches on the radio. On the CBC, a program about a native tribe up north. There's nothing written down, no alphabet, and the youngest person to speak the language is eighty-six. An old woman speaks in a clucking accent: "When I die, the language will be lost."

Lena turns the radio off. What is it with the CBC and these stories of loss? What is it with Canadians and history? They hunger for it but, in the end, it's never glamorous enough. They want the Alamo and Graceland, not burls and Indians.

When she was new to this country, Lena was constantly asking herself, "Is this what it means to be Canadian? Is this?" She would pick the most Canadian girl in the room and study her, memorizing how to be: friendly but distant; jokey but sad; humble on the outside, proud on the inside. Was it as easy as acting like a boy but dressing like a girl? Was it a combination of talking a lot and apologizing often? Years later, when she still couldn't quite put her finger on what it was that made these girls more Canadian than her, she decided it didn't have anything to do with anything. She decided you just had to be born here and pretend it mattered.

But now, having spent the day driving through the pretty lake-view parts of Ontario and the crusty moonscape parts and the car lot/strip mall parts; having seen so much Ontario she has had to re-evaluate her concept of the universe, her place in it, the meaning of things, she's start-ing to think maybe this place does affect people. All that driving and yet, when she finally pulls over at a motel next to the highway she finds she is still—*still!*—in Ontario.

IT'S ONLY ONCE she's paid for her room that Lena notices the hotel has been taken over by some sort of youth lead-ership summit. Everywhere she looks, future leaders are roaming the hallways in neon shirts. In the lobby she comes across a group trying to build an elaborate bridge using toothpicks and bubble gum. By the elevator another group is lisping softly about physics and schisms and time-space continuums.

Lena is plodding down the hall, feeling like the woman from Ama's story, like a thousand-pound statue of herself, when she gets stopped by two adults with clipboards and headsets.

"Say now, aren't you that museum lady?" the woman asks.

"Actually, there is no more 'Museum—'" Lena starts.

"It is!" the man points. "It's you!"

Ben and Jill introduce themselves as fifth-grade teachers, but Lena can already tell. They're all amped up like fifth-grade teachers and are wondering if she would be willing to give her "Shoebox Museum" talk. They practically beg so Lena does what any Great Canadian would.

"DID YOU KNOW that long ago the first museums were started by kings and queens?" Lena asks a room full of fifth-graders later that evening.

The students don't respond but Ben and Jill give her a pair of perfectly synchronized thumbs-up from the back of the room.

"Back then you either had to be very wealthy or very lucky to enter a museum," Lena continues. "But nowadays we can all go to museums and for a very reasonable price too!"

The students stare blankly at her or past her, it's hard to say.

She tells them museums were once called Cabinets of *Curiosity*! Cabinets of *Wonder*! Memory *Theatres*! "Think about that," she says, "Memory! Theatre!" Here she uses something like jazz hands to generate excitement.

But these future leaders are impervious to jazz hands. They don't even flinch.

Lena tells them that museums are humanity's best defence against grief and loss and the cruel passage of time, that without museums we can't have a truly tactile experience of our past, and without experiencing our past we can't possibly know who we are, we can't possibly build a future. Her voice wobbles, just a little.

The kids hang their heads in shame or boredom, she can't say.

"Even a website is a kind of museum!" she says, brightening. "Even Facebook, in a way!"

Here, finally, the kids look up.

Lena quickly pulls out the "specialty" items she's excavated from the back of her trunk for this, her final appearance as the "Museum Lady." First, an assortment of kidney stones in a velvet case—some smooth as beach rock, some bumpy as coral, some brightly swirled like a glass marble, or with intricate floral patterns. Next, she brings out a collection of monkey skulls, one inside another, smaller and smaller, like nesting dolls, and says that there's no explanation for how they got that way. She pulls out the jaw of a shark, a brain in a bottle and an unidentifiable petrified sea creature—half turtle, half seahorse.

Just like Lena suspected, the kids are fascinated. They're up out of their seats to gawk at the kidney stones. They rattle the monkey skulls and shake the brain in the bottle. They take turns placing the shark jaw over their heads.

Ben and Jill look at each other with alarm.

Standing at their centre, Lena gestures for the kids to pull into a tight huddle and then asks how many have visited a museum this year. She gets the usual spray of hands. She asks which museums and gets the usual answers: the Wax Museum, Science World, Miniature World, Butterfly World. She instructs them that wax can't teach us anything about the past, that butterflies belong in parks and that they should be deeply suspicious of any place claiming to be a "World." She bangs her fist on the table top, but not in a frightening way.

Ben and Jill are now bouncing up on their tippy-toes at the edge of the huddle, trying to see what's going on.

Lena quickly showers the kids with fliers from local museums—the Museum of Bait and Tackle, the Button Museum, the Mustard Museum, the Antique Hammer Museum. She explains that one-point-five of these museums close their doors every week because not enough kids are interested in real history. She says that every time one of these museums closes its doors for good it is a small death for the country, a small death for history, for mankind. She is yelling, but just a little, and only because she cares.

Ben and Jill are now clapping their hands trying to break up the crowd.

"Think about that," Lena says. "Small. Death. You want that on your conscience the rest of your life?" Her hands are shaking.

At this point Ben thanks Lena loudly as Jill claims her spot at the front of the room to explain the "shoebox museum project" they are about to embark on.

Lena places the rest of her pamphlets on the nearest table. Then she packs up her kidney stones and skulls, goes out to her car and, for the first time in decades, has a real grown-up cry.

BACK ON THE ROAD, with every station playing either Joni Mitchell or Leonard Cohen—all those high-highs and low-lows—Lena thinks back to the museum that got her started on this cross-Canada journey—the Michael Dunlop Memorial Museum. If anyone can be said to have vanished into thin air, it's Michael Dunlop. He was abducted in broad daylight from a playground half a block from his house. In grief and in hope, Michael's mother did the only thing she could: she gathered and organized every little thing relating to her son—every drawing and piece of writing, every photograph and home movie—and started a museum. She made lists of his favourite foods and colours and animals and teams. She documented his first and last words, first and last days of school, first and last birthdays and put all of these things on display for the public. From a distance it seemed desperate, but after visiting, you could understand why she had done it. You couldn't spend an hour in that room without feeling you had known the boy and, for the rest of your life, looking twice at every lonely kid with his ball cap pulled down low.

Driving into that part of Manitoba that is like being cradled in the palm of a hand, against that pure white backdrop, Lena can't help but fill her own memory theatre.

Her and Ama's first and only plane ride together: the way Ama gripped her seat and whimpered during takeoff; how, after she finished her meal, she carried her tray to the back and tried to do her own dishes; how she spent most of the flight sneaking stray cutlery and peanuts and sugar packets into her dress pockets, then, when the flight attendants invited them to visit the cockpit, as was the custom in those days, she stood trembling and crying before the handsome pilots, convinced they were going to throw her off the plane for stealing.

Those first days in Canada: the two of them rolling English words in their mouths like camels, blushing and staring at their hands every time someone asked them where they were from or how they were doing.

Their first apartment by the side of the highway: how suspicious they were of the fridge that shivered and the pipes that groaned and the lights that buzzed; how odd that a place could be so quiet and so loud at once.

Their first doctor's appointment: they were diagnosed with PTSD and given pills, pills, pills—a whole bag full of samples—but as soon as they stepped outside, Ama threw those pills into the nearest Dumpster saying only, "We don't have the *Psssst*." It was the last time either of them saw a doctor for decades.

Their first TV set: stuck on the children's channel for months because they didn't know there were other channels; when Ama stepped on the remote and accidentally changed to the women's channel for the first time, the two of them stared open-mouthed at what they saw. Women in dresses and heels. Women in bed. Women in bars. Women with guns. Naked women. Policewomen.

How amazed they were, that first winter, by the snow so deep people had to dig tunnels to their cars, by the air so cold it froze their eyelashes together. That was the winter Ama put a homemade sign with a picture of a sewing machine up in the window. Clients would come in to have their hems and cuffs measured but before long they'd be telling Ama all their problems and offering up their palms. Within a year Ama had a thriving psychic business. "Canadians," Ama used to joke, "hem their pants and they tell you everything."

LENA HAS BEEN driving through the Prairies for days. She has seen so much horizon and listened to so much CBC, she is on the verge of deciding that it really *does* mean something to be Canadian, that is has to do with heading all the way west and losing your mother or mother tongue or motherland, also something to do with knowing who you are not more than who you are, something to do with feeling your bigness and your smallness at once—when Ama calls.

"Ama, where are you?" Lena shouts.

"Jastrebarsko," Ama says.

"Jastra-*who*-sko?" Lena asks.

In the background Lena can hear people yelling in the old language, arguing about the price of something. In the distance, she hears the clanging of pots and pans, dogs barking, a church bell. It all sounds distinctly un-Canadian.

"Ama, what's going on? Are you at a movie theatre?" Up ahead she notices a strip of black cloud squatting low over the road.

"I'm back home," Ama says.

"What do you mean, *back*?"

"Old country," Ama says.

The world pitches and whirls around Lena's head, spun off its centre. Up ahead, those black clouds are roiling. "But I thought there was no *back*," she says. "I thought home was here, in Canada."

"Your home," Ama says. Then she coughs, wet and loose, like she's drowning in glue.

All the air rushes out of Lena's body as she recalls another fairy tale Ama once told, about an old woman who walked all the way home to die among her people.

Lena crumples over the steering wheel, momentarily hollow. Her stomach contracts. Her heart stretches out. So this is grief, she thinks. It is Canada-sized, a feeling so big it threatens to smother her.

"Lena, I must go," Ama says. "They make a party for me."

Lena thinks of Burt who vanished one piece at a time, of Michael Dunlop who was gone in an instant. "Wait, Ama," she says, "what happened the day the soldiers came? How did we escape? Did I hide really well?" Her words echo down the line—small, growing smaller.

"Not you," Ama says. "Little Yakov. Your brother."

It's hard to say if those clouds are barrelling down on Lena or if she's just driving straight into them.

"All day they made him run in circles," Ama says. "And when he fell, they shooted."

Lena can suddenly understand why a person would choose to live here as the only spot of colour in such a vast white land. At least out here you can see things coming.

"I don't understand," Lena says. "Where was I?"

Ama's breath is scraping in, scraping out. "You came later," she says. "After."

Lena can't tell where she is in relation to the road any-more. It's snowing up and down and sideways and in curtains. Her car is briefly airborne, the dashboard a con-stellation of lights.

"After what?" she asks, but Ama is coughing. In the back-ground, the village dogs are going wild.

"Ha!" Ama says. "The dogs, they think I barking!" Then the phone cuts out. The car shudders and dies.

Lena steps out of the car, loose and herky-jerky, like a skeleton from a closet. Inching forward into all that white on white on white is like walking into static, only it bites her skin and whistles in her ears. She could float away in a wind like this, she thinks. She could shatter and scatter, to fall as bad weather somewhere far, far away. She heads toward an orange light in the distance, thinking of Yakov, the brother she never knew, of Ama led on a rope leash by her father. Then the ground gives way and she is up to her waist in a snowdrift. She can no longer move, but she doesn't mind. *What could be more Canadian than this?* she thinks. The snow whips at her and she doesn't mind that either. Her father was a bad man with a gun. She is a bad daughter who insisted on knowing. So let her be whipped. Let her fade away, as Canadian as a lost song, as a language without an alphabet.

LENA WAKES IN A crisp hospital bed. Right away a nurse is there to tell her she may never again have sensation below the ankles, but she is very lucky to be alive. The nurse reaches for a clipboard and arches her eyebrows way up as if she is about to say something startling or wonderful when Lena's phone rings.

She fumbles for it. "Ama? Where are you?"

"I here," Ama says. "Home. Petrovska." Her breathing sounds like slippers dragged across a hardwood floor.

Lena tells Ama about wandering into the storm, about the snowdrift and how she may never feel her feet again. She tells Ama she's no longer the "Museum Lady," that her future is just like a prairie in a snowstorm—a blank white page and she has no idea how to fill it. Then she does what she has never done. She asks if Ama would, just this once, look into her future and tell her what she sees.

But Ama can't. Or she won't. Instead she tells a story of that first airplane ride so long ago, specifically of the moment they stood in the cockpit, with the thousand lights and dials and the clouds sliding over the nose of the airplane. She says at that moment she felt her entire past drop away, that her stomach became suddenly light and swimmy—a feeling she would later learn to describe as hope.

Lena is silent, trying to draw the connections.

"Everything, already you know," Ama says. "Follow your nose!"

"Isn't that a line from a cereal commercial?" Lena asks.

"I mean," Ama says, gentler now, "follow your senses. You will know the way."

But Lena isn't so sure. When asked to list all of the senses once on a second-grade quiz, she filled the page: *thinking, knowing, not knowing, crying, singing, remembering, forgetting*... And the last time she thought she knew the way, she ended up in a snowdrift.

"Lena, I must go," Ama says. "I feel like old goat."

Lena can only imagine what they do with old goats in Petrovska, so they say their goodbyes. When she hangs up the nurse is there, still with those eyebrows.

"I have some news for you, if now's a good time!" she says.

WHEN AMA CALLS next, Lena is out of the hospital and driving through the Rockies.

She pulls over at a rest stop with a view as if from the top of the world and tells Ama she is pregnant, that there was one time before, but this time she's keeping it, she's going home to B.C.

"Oh my Lena!" Ama says and then there is a thud, like a sack of potatoes hitting the ground. Lena hears the phone swing on its cord, hitting the stool once, twice, and then

Ama is gone. It isn't a sound that lets her know so much as a change in the air—something lost. Lena stays on the phone. She would give anything to know the look on Ama's face—whether it's a smile or a frown, shock or grace.

Finally, she hears a man approach. "Rosie, Rosie," he says. He is weeping, kissing her. Who is this man who loves Ama so much? She hears him call for help and then the commotion of a small crowd gathering. Finally someone picks up.

"Lena? Lena, my God," a woman says in English. Then in the old language: "Our Rosalie has gone around the corner." Lena remembers now: in the old country people don't die, they just go up ahead a little ways, just out of sight.

She stays on the line while the woman, Mrs. Valdovsky, updates her: now the men are back with a blanket; now they're putting the coins over her eyes; now they're lifting her; now they're carrying her up the hill. She can picture the village, the hill, the men with their shovels. She can't picture Ama's face, but she's too afraid to ask.

"Can you come?" Mrs. Valdovsky asks once Ama has disappeared over the hill. But they both know Ama would want to be buried quickly, that it's the old-world way.

"No, Mrs. Valdovsky, I can't," Lena says.

"Is okay," she says, in English now. "We make special here."

And so, while the men go off to prepare the grave, the women hold a makeshift ceremony. Lena imagines them standing in a circle as they pass the phone. Each person takes a turn saying how happy Ama seemed, how proud she was, how much she loved Lena. Then, they share a memory of Ama before she was Ama—how she once wrestled a runaway pig to the ground with her bare hands, the time she pretended to be a boy so she could enter an arm-wrestling competition, how she was the only girl to ever court men, leaving anonymous flowers on their windowsills at night.

"Ama did that?" Lena asks.

"Rosalie did," they say. In death she is Rosalie.

When it's time for Ama to be buried, the whole village gathers around the phone to say a prayer. They sing a high, whining song and then say their goodbyes. They are off to bury Ama.

It is then, alone again—or for the first time—and with the world laid out like a blueprint far below, that Lena can sense her future. It's a feeling inside, a holding on and a spreading out, like a perfect April potato taking root. It is fluttery like fear and swimmy like hope. She puts her car into gear and follows her nose down the long steep hill toward home.

Walking into Ama's apartment for the first time in years, the air is so close and sweet and full of Ama, Lena has to check all the rooms and closets just to be sure she isn't hiding somewhere. She doesn't find Ama but when she walks into the spare bedroom and finds a crib piled high with baby clothes, she knows everything she needs to know. Above the crib a homemade banner reads, *Is a Girl!* in sparkly pink writing—it's Ama's final psychic act, one last "Ha!" from beyond the grave, or just up ahead, as the case may be.

refugee love

JOINING THE FIRST floor of Human Capital Inc., the second largest staffing firm in the city, was the only thing that could've saved me. It was the late eighties, the end of a naïve and dramatic decade, and I'd been dumped more times than I could count on all my fingers and all my toes. But at Human Capital, at least I wasn't alone.

We were all women on our floor, all wounded, disappointed and on the wrong side of thirty, which is why we'd been hired. We were skeptical and jaded in all the right ways. We could home in on inconsistencies and half-truths like lawyers or mothers. Not only that, we had the perfect Human Resources smiles—smiles that showed exactly ten teeth, that were exactly as warm as they were cold. We were killers and yet—as dictated by the men upstairs (the men who ran the show)—we were not allowed to deviate from the twenty-five-question intake interview script. Not under any circumstances. We were to wade through the chaff and send all the promising candidates upstairs for the "real, in-depth interviewing." That was the eighties for you. All our shoulder pads and trendy blazers couldn't hide the fact that we were women living in a man's world.

No one knows who started it, which woman was the first to arrive at the end of Human Capital's twenty-five-question intake interview, look at the man across from her and decide *Fuck it. Let's do this.* I heard stories about a red-headed, big-bosomed woman named Judy Jefferson. People said she was thrice divorced—a real tigress—and looking for a fourth. Or she'd had a string of bad first dates. Or she'd just been dumped. Rumour is she reached into her desk one day—while shaking out her hair or kicking off her heels, depending on which version of the story you heard—pulled out her own private list of yearning, burning questions, cleared her throat, and started in on number 26. Whoever Judy was, whatever her reasons, by the time I arrived on the first floor of Human Capital Inc., we were all following in her footsteps.

Those were the days. We did our regular work when the bosses were looking and "Judy's work" when they turned away. There were always strapping single men wandering the hallways, back for third and fourth interviews. "I'm here for the Jefferson Account?" they'd say, waving their appointment slip timidly. Someone was always working through lunch with the blinds to her interoffice windows snapped tight. Someone was always wearing leather or leopard print or strappy stilettos. The perfume was thick, the pheromones thicker, but the men upstairs never said a word. Either they didn't care or we ran a good cover.

REFUGEE LOVE

Can you blame us for making the most of an opportunity? Back then there was no such thing as online dating, no appropriate venue for a thorough grilling. It was all blind dates, singles bars and personal ads, all fumble and error. If we developed strategies, it was only to protect ourselves. If we got carried away, it was only a symptom of the times. In the eighties, putting a desk between you and a man, having him squirm in the interview seat, may have been the only way to get the upper hand.

We took Judy's work very seriously. It took great skill to lead a man through a detailed history of his dating life in a way that reassured him, *Yes, these are actual Human Capital questions.* Much science went into the scenario portion of our interviews—adultery scenarios, marriage scenarios, fatherhood scenarios. Our dream analysis was solid, our personality predictors as accurate as possible for the times.

Over the years I learned to spot an egomaniac the moment he sat down. It was all in the posture. If he sat like he thought he was Buddha, I wouldn't waste another second. I threw him to the boys upstairs and tried not to get any on me.

I knew the Peter Pans by their bright eyes and quick jokes, but our statistics didn't lie: they were always looking for a mother figure.

And I knew the victim types by their cowlicks and coffee stains, by the way they seemed to jitter at the slightest provocation, like the filament inside a light bulb. It would have been easy to fool myself into thinking, *Now here's a safe bet. Someone I can take home and smother,* but I knew it was just a matter of time until all that tension blew sky high.

All those interviews, all that inquiry, but nothing could have prepared me for the refugee lover.

I'D BEEN AT Human Capital a few years, interviewing for the "Jefferson Account" for nearly as long, when I first met Paolo. I was as ruthless and skilled as the rest of them. So what if I kept notebooks with the specific qualities I was looking for in a mate? So I wrote down a few of my romantic fantasies, made a few collages of swarthy men on sailboats, shirtless men on beaches—is that such a grave tactical error?

Our interview must've started with the usual: schools attended, best and worst qualities, extracurricular activities, but looking at his file now, I see I didn't take notes. I'm sure I stumbled over his name—Paul-oh? *Pow-low,* he would've corrected—his name so round and seductive when spoken aloud. I probably inquired about his accent—Mexican? *Argentine,* he would've explained. All of this must've led to some discussion about his visa status.

I remember him fidgeting in his seat, looking at the little scrap of paper in his hand, and asking, "Isn't this the Day Labour Office?"

"That's on the third floor, sweetpea," I said, "but you're here now so let's do this. You and me: a real tête-à-tête."

I was trying to act casual but I'd already noticed he had the posture of a question mark, hairy knuckles and the kindest face I'd ever seen—everything wide open, everything full moon and yearning upwards. I remember thinking these were both my favourite things about him and the things I most wanted to change.

We eventually reached the interpretive portion of the interview, "Gateway Questions," designed to separate the spontaneous thinkers from the drones. Human Capital was big on the interpretive in the eighties: *If you were a tree/ animal/vegetable, what kind would you be?* Here so many interviewees would relax and say the first thing to come into their heads. Normally there was nothing I could do to help the weeping willows, the pandas, the tomatoes. But it just so happened we were in the middle of a big hiring push. *Company-wide lowering of standards,* the office-memo had read that morning.

"Avocado," Paolo said.

Creamy, wholesome, deceptive middle, I wrote in his file.

I tapped my pencil three times, part of General Intimidation—*Never forget you are in an interview,* the corporate literature read. *Never allow the client to get comfortable. Remain skeptical, distant, judgmental.*

I had a soft spot for this man before me. Here was a fresh-faced immigrant, so far from home, so alone, wearing someone else's corduroy jacket—too small in the shoulders, too big in the collar. I could rename him, take him shopping, teach him dirty words. I could mould him into whomever I wanted. The thought of having to send him upstairs made my stomach swim.

"I've got just the placement for you," I said, reaching into my desk, "but the Jefferson Account will require extensive interviewing."

Question 26. Some days it was a conundrum—*Your lover is burning down. What parts of her do you save?* Some days it was a challenge—*I am the last woman on earth. You have thirty seconds to convince me to mate.* And other days it was just a fragment—*I need . . .*

I read what was at the top of my list: "If you could save just one word from the English language"—not my best work, but I was still figuring things out in those days.

I recall he didn't ask, "Why just one word?" or "Save it from what?" the way other interviewees did that day. He just leaned forward, lifted one corner of his mouth and with a confidence unimpeded by his corduroy jacket said, "If. *If* is the best word."

His Adam's apple dipping and bobbing. His puddle-brown eyes. How I wanted to splash in those puddles. How I wanted to make a mess of him and then tidy him up again.

It is, to this day, the most romantic interview I've had. How he teared up during the family values segment, the way he described his mother, the vulnerable self-portrait he drew—the foreshortened limbs, the fact that he forgot to draw feet—I still have it framed on my desk.

At the end of it all, he wiped the tears from his eyes and asked me out.

There would be no copying down his address, no "bumping into him" at various hotspots in his neighbourhood—the way we used to in those days. There would be no need to stage a follow-up interview.

"Feliz hora?" he said.

Happy Hour. I couldn't believe my luck.

IF. "IF" WAS a sweet little game we all liked to play in the eighties: *if* he hadn't stumbled into the wrong office that day, *if* I hadn't got my hands on his paperwork before he realized his mistake, *if* I hadn't stunned him and then worked him into a corner with my questions, *if* he hadn't been so gentle and awkward, *if* I hadn't been so well-trained—what then? Would we have met some other way? Would the fate fairies have twinkled down on little wings and somehow rearranged time and space to bring us together?

DECEMBER IS A month for catching colds on purpose so you can call in sick and worm around in bed. It is a month for peeling one orange after another and not even eating them, just sticking your nose into the heaps of peel on your bedside table and remembering warmer times. It is a month to turn up the heat and drink sangria in bed while recalling your best sunburn ever, your worst mosquito bite, and feeling you'd give anything to have your blood airborne just now. It is all of this, but it's a dangerous month to fall in love, a dangerous time of year to turn to one another and say, "Why pay two rents when we could pay one?" December weakens us, makes us foolish and sentimental. I know this now, but I didn't know it then.

In December he moved in. It was a decision based on necessity more than romance. We hadn't even slept together yet, but his roommate, Escobar, had forgotten to pay the rent three months in a row and Paolo had nowhere else to go. "But I still want to go slow," he insisted, placing his four boxes at the back of my closet.

I bought new sheets, faked a thyroid condition and said I'd be working from home that week, administrative work and follow-up calls.

We had complete disregard for time of day. We stayed up late "getting to know each other," making out, watching movies. I'd never met a man like this before. He wanted to know all about my childhood, my secrets, my heartbreaks. He was big on lists: top three biggest crushes, top five best days of my life, top ten worst fears. He wanted to play Truth or Dare and Twenty Questions into the early morning. Half the time it felt like he was interviewing me. I'd never felt so hopeful, so weak in the knees. We ate at midnight and slept into the afternoon. He drew pictures of me while I slept. I'd find them stuck to the fridge later with little poems attached. He insisted on painting my toenails. He'd meet me just out of the tub with a new bottle in hand, saying only, "Ravishing Red." I'd pretend to be coy—"Who me?"—and then he'd tackle. It was the most wonderful, epic foreplay I'd had in years. I felt like a teenager, like a princess, like an exotic and extremely ripe fruit. Then he sat me down and explained that he wanted to wait until we were seriously committed to make love. "It's a religious thing," he said. Then, "Do you want to play Twenty Questions again?" I agreed, because it was my number one all-time favourite game but also because I was confident I could break him.

He started to talk about the future a lot—*our* future. We would flip through lifestyle magazines, nailing down the details of our dream home. "Do you like window seats?" he'd ask. "Carpet or wood flooring?" He even started making collages: vacation spots, home furnishings, his and hers clothing, cars, espresso machines.

Looking back, something in me should have sat up alert at all this, but it was around this time he turned to me and said it, the actual word, out loud.

"Love," he said. He screwed the cap back on the Ravishing Red, looked at me, into me. "I think I'm in love."

Some parts of me fluttered. Some other parts ached.

It's not that I was surprised. I'd been checking the love line on my palm for changes and every morning it seemed redder, deeper, truer. I had been smiling at the chest hairs in my bathroom sink, using Crest when I really preferred Colgate, eating pizza even though I was lactose intolerant. I had let him have the better pillow. Why all this making way if I wasn't in love too? Why else this giving over of palms so that things could be written there?

But *love* was a word I was unaccustomed to hearing from the mouths of men. It was such a taboo word in the dating world back then, we of the first floor had undergone extensive hypnotherapy to erase it from our vocabularies entirely. And yet, here was a man saying it with such intention, the same way he'd slid his tattered blue Bible onto my bookshelf, the same way he moved through a room, planting each footstep solidly as if it were the only thing holding him to the earth. I wanted to say it back, but I couldn't. It went against all of my training. It was the third most romantic moment of my life, but I couldn't quite participate.

I took another week off work. We stayed indoors. He followed me room to room, composing songs on his ukulele, offering to wash and braid my hair, painting and repainting my toes, but still no sex. Eventually, when the only food left in the house was a watermelon, I went to put my shoes on. I was feeling bug-eyed, twitchy, with an itch I couldn't scratch.

"Why do you leave me?" he asked.

"Just getting some food," I answered.

At that, he picked up the watermelon and smashed it against the floor. "But we have food right here!" He slurped the meat rather than cutting into it the regular way. "Fruit should be an experience," he said, sucking up seeds from his leg hair. I knew he was South American but this was the moment I *believed* it.

It wasn't until the next day that I finally got my chance to slip away to the corner store. Enough with the fruit and foreplay! I needed a moment alone and also some beef jerky. I needed to reconnect with my training. *Every client has a past,* the corporate literature read. *Never let the client run away with the interview.*

"Listen," I said when I got back to our lair. "I need to know about your past, so give me the bad news and give it to me straight. What's your damage?"

I noticed he had lit a whole bunch of candles while I was out, that he'd covered the floor with what looked like tea but was actually dried rose petals. The whole place smelled like singed grass.

"I have no past. I have only the future," he said, and I'll admit they were words I'd waited all my life to hear.

That's when it happened.

He got down on one knee. "A wise man once said to me, only a fool rushes into love," he said. "But I just can't help falling in love with you." He produced a ring from behind his back. "Please give me your hand, but give me your whole life too. I just can't help falling in love with you—"

"You just said that," I interrupted.

"Please will you marry me?" he said

Something in me went *splat:* the second most romantic moment of my life.

My answer: "Does that mean we can have sex now?"

His answer: "Let's wait until the honeymoon" and "What's a couple of weeks compared to a lifetime?"

"Okay, okay. Yes, yes, yes," I said, because the eighties had been a long, hard decade and I was staring down a diamond and even a killer can lose her focus when she's face-to-face with the prize. After all, I had cracked the code, found the loophole. I couldn't wait to tell the girls at work. Immigrants for all! Puppy love for everyone!

"UN-*FUCKING*-BELIEVABLE!" Faith said, fluffing her perm. We were standing in the first-floor bathroom. "You asked him about his past and he *proposed!*"

"He said 'love,' and you haven't even had *sex!*" said Ginger, hiking up her nylons.

"That is *so* totally romantic!" Tiffany said, hairspraying her bangs.

Then they started in with the questions:

Faith: "Is he gay? Check if his fingernails are manicured."

Ginger: "Is he an ex-con? Check if his clothes are way out of style."

Tiffany: "How did he propose? Was it *so* romantic?"

I told them the story. How a wise old man once told Paolo that only a fool would rush into love—

"Wait, aren't those Elvis lyrics?" Faith interrupted. She started humming. They all did. Crooning Paolo's proposal to some tune they all knew.

"'Only Fools Rush In.' It *is* an Elvis song," said Ginger. "My parents had their first dance to that song."

"Wait. That doesn't make it any less romantic, does it?" asked Tiffany. "Maybe he's never heard the song."

"Maybe he's a whole new type," Faith said, spraying perfume into the air and ducking under it, "working a whole new angle we've never seen before."

All four of us looked at each other, inhaled, choked on perfume.

THE NEXT FEW weeks Paolo chased me around the house asking me endless wedding questions. He'd been to the immigration office to get something called a fiancé visa and was a little overexcited. We lived in one of those fifties-style apartments where all the rooms open onto one another. I would come home from work and he'd follow me from the kitchen to the dining room to the living room to the bedroom to the bathroom, calling his questions after me: "Indoor or outdoor?" he wanted to know. "Winter or spring? Tiered cake or slab cake?"

"What's that?" I'd call back. "I can't hear you."

NEAR THE END of January, Mum called with a whole new lineup. A dentist and a banker. A lawyer and a realtor. One was a widower, which might've been tempting once.

"No can do," I said.

"What does that mean, sweetie? Speak properly."

"Means I'm busy, Mum. Like, marathon busy."

Paolo had finally caught up to me and was leaning in the door frame, listening.

He pointed to the wedding magazine in his hand and mouthed, "Tell her." Those full-moon eyes, his pouty shoulders.

I broke it to Mum as slowly as possible, in a roundabout way, but it didn't help. "Paul-*who?*" she screeched.

"Pow-low," I corrected.

"Po-elo," she said. "Aren't things moving a bit *fast?* Shouldn't we *meet* him first? You *know* your father's not very good with accents."

"Like this, Mum: Pow-low. And it's not too fast."

"Paul-oh," she said. "Oh dear. I just saw a movie about this. He isn't looking for citizenship is he? Is *that* what the rush is all about?" Her questions were ice cubes. They chilled and then stung and then numbed.

"Just call him Paul," I said. "Paul is fine."

THAT NIGHT WHILE Paolo called around to different wedding venues, I pulled my old notebooks down from my highest bookshelves. What I found there, in amongst the descriptions of my dream partner, the lists of "Top Ten Most Romantic Gestures" and "Five Best Proposals Ever," made the skin under my engagement ring itch. *Not afraid to speak of the future. Unconventional, exotic,* I had written. *Paints toes, plays with hair—not just after sex.* There was even a photo of a shirtless Hawaiian man serenading a woman with a ukulele, even an article about a sweet Russian couple who'd saved themselves until marriage. I couldn't believe what I was reading. I had wanted this once. I had dreamed Paolo long ago, down to every last detail and now he had appeared.

THE NEXT MORNING I made Paolo drag his four boxes out from the back of my closet. We were sitting on my bedroom floor—speechless, surrounded by old photos, books, letters and diaries, everything in Spanish and coated in thick South American dust—when the phone started to ring. We sat upright, like squirrels sensing a storm. Our eyes locked onto each other for four whole rings before the machine picked up. Then Mum's voice filled the apartment.

"Listen, honey, this Paul-oh. I just didn't have a good feeling so I called a lawyer. It doesn't look good. Call me back."

"So you *do* have a past?" I said looking at Paolo's belongings all around us.

My finger had swollen up overnight—red and tight under my ring. *Of course* he had a past. *Every* man has a past: it was the number one rule. I was used to a long line of exes stretching off into the distance, winking and waving like the bitches they are, each having left her mark, the different dents and bruises that made up the man before me—we of the first floor had ways of dealing with exes—but this was something else.

He reached across and squeezed my hand. "More importantly, I have a future," he said. I wanted to believe him, but my mother was still in the air.

REFUGEE LOVE

I interrogated him further while he continued to unpack. He told me about Buenos Aires, a crumbling city with a grand old history. "Disrepair is so much more beautiful than perfection," he said. The buildings there were organized into impenetrable city blocks locked off from the street but for a single door, he said. On the other side of that door, a long dark hallway led to the very centre of the *manzana*, or apple, as the blocks were called.

I was trying to locate myself in this anecdote. Was he the apple? Was I the worm? I was confused. Were we disrepair or perfection?

The phone was ringing again. Mum: she would call and call until she got an answer.

To a foreigner out on the street, the city might seem abandoned, he said, but at the centre of each *manzana* lay an open square of green, the *pulmón,* or lung. That's where families breathed. Women cooked and children chased dogs and old men stared at the sun, spitting sunflower seeds. He said that from a rooftop you could look out and see all those *pulmónes* as wild bursts of green amidst so much concrete.

I was starting to understand. In every man's past there is that *one,* the girl who divided his life into a before and after, the "Supreme Bitch" we the women of the first floor liked to call her.

"Remember, we are always competing with her," we reminded each other. As staff of the second-largest hiring firm, we were in a position to run background checks on the Supreme Bitch. We could call her employer and references, or if she lived in the city, we could just stand outside her apartment and see for ourselves. We always knew exactly what we were up against.

But this Supreme Bitch wasn't a woman. She was the motherland and she had broken him long before anyone was keeping track. I was perfection and she was disrepair. I was modern, plain and tall, and she had the slow curves of history. How could I compete?

"These asylum seekers," Mum said into the answering machine, "they're not *legal,* honey, not until they've passed this test—" there was the shuffling of paper—"this 'Credible Fear Screening.' They've actually got to have a certain amount of *fear* about going back where they came from. And *sometimes* if there isn't enough fear, they just find someone quick to marry." She stayed on the line, exhaling.

"So you're saying you want to go back there?" I asked. "It's sexier there? You wish you'd never left? How can it be sexier there if you weren't having sex?"

He was ripping into his last box, Styrofoam peanuts spilling everywhere when he said there was no reason to go back, that his whole family was "disappeared."

"What do you mean *disappeared?* Just into thin air?"

"Nobody knows. Some say thrown into the river," he said.

The very idea made me mad. I much preferred closure.

He lifted a huge wooden shield from the box. Styrofoam shrieked all around us. The shield was the size of his torso, the wood so old it looked like it had been coated in tar. He twirled it around to face me. I took one look at the shrunken black head mounted there; Mum hung up and I fainted.

REFUGEE LOVE

When I came to he was quick with the explanations. "It's not what you think," he said, and then explained that it was a family heirloom, a sea tortoise from his grandfather's shipping days.

I could see it then—the small beaky nose, the turned-down mouth, those sad lidded eyes. Not human. Not an old man's head shellacked and mounted to a plaque in my hallway, looking like it so badly needed a drink. More like a nailed-down worm.

"Maybe we should get that," I croaked.

"Get what?"

"The phone."

But the phone wasn't ringing anymore, only in my head.

He brought me water and then told me a sad story about his uncles being taken in the night, how his family was ejected so quickly from the upper-middle class that his mother had to sell off the family heirlooms one by one, how she finally died of grief. This tortoise head was the one thing she hadn't sold, the last family relic.

My limbs were tingling back to life. "So are you *really* afraid to go back there, or just a little afraid?" I asked. "And where'd you get the ring? Did you buy it before you moved in? Before you even knew me?"

He sputtered, puffing and waving his hands through the air.

In the end, I let him mount the tortoise above the TV. After all he'd been through I wanted him to feel at home. Every time I looked up at it though, I was reminded that his life was divided not just into a before and after, but also a here and there. I was reminded that I was the foreigner out on the empty street, banging on the door, wanting to be let into the *pulmón*, to breathe at the centre of things.

THERE WAS NO MORE avoiding it. It was time to meet my parents.

On our way out of the city we stopped at three different specialty shops looking for the right pot of jam. It had to be apricot, the right colour and consistency, with a smallish label. It had to be American. It couldn't be French or Italian.

Once we were on the road I explained how Dad refused to wear his hearing aid. I told Paolo about the help, not to help the help. I explained that our jam would be placed on a shelf with all the other jams in the summer kitchen, that this was *display* jam, not to be confused with the other *regular* jam.

He started to say, "Where I come from—" but his voice was cancelled out by a big rig passing in the next lane. I can only assume he ended the sentence with something like "Kids line up outside the door just to lick the empty jars." *Where I come from* was a sentence that never ended well. I turned up the music. If we had a fight now, it would trail us like a bad smell and Mum would detect it as soon as we walked in the door.

For the rest of the ride I heard him rehearsing under his breath. "Tell me, do you have many friends in the country?" and "I hear your roses won third place at the county fair" and "May I ask what's in the soup?"

MY PARENTS BURST out of the dining room in a stampede of poodles. I had forgotten to warn Paolo about the dogs.

REFUGEE LOVE

Mum had him backed into a corner and agreeing to be "just Paul" in no time. It was then I noticed he was wearing that old corduroy jacket from our first interview along with matching pants that were hemmed too short. He looked out of place and time—a used car salesman suddenly beamed into my parents' marble foyer.

Since it was a beautiful day, we were going to eat out in the summer kitchen—a peachy turret detached from the rest of the house and the place where Mum kept her jam collection. It was arranged on shelves in front of the tall windows, creating a stained-glass effect.

We were still talking about the weather, about the fresh coat of paint and how much the jam collection had grown, when Paolo barked: "Do you have friends in the country?" His accent was as thick and gooey as the light. Fortunately, neither of them heard. I patted his leg under the table. Bad timing was all. I'd forgotten about the acoustics out there, how the high ceilings swallowed sound.

I waited until we were all settled and then repeated his question at a more appropriate volume, without the accent.

"Well, of course," Mum said looking at me. She rested her hand on her collarbone. "*All* our friends are American."

I was just about to clear up the misunderstanding—country*side* not country—when Maria came in with the soup. Paolo could hardly look at her. He just bowed his head and kept it there. She was probably his mother's age.

"So, Paul, were things extremely *bad* in your homeland?" Mum asked while Maria dished the soup. "Is *that* why you came to the United States of America?"

"Mum!" I said. "Jesus!"

"Language?" she said.

The soup was served. Maria backed out of the room.

"Isn't this soup *lovely?*" Mum said, changing tack.

"Yes, it's a very lovely soup," I said.

"Lovely soup for a lovely day," Dad said.

We all swallowed: one, two, three.

"May I ask what's in the soup?" Paolo asked, but he sounded like he'd just woken from a deep sleep, like his mouth wasn't working properly and he didn't look up when he said it, as if he were asking the soup itself.

Nobody responded.

"The goat cheese is lovely, too," Mum said next. "And these olives are from—"

"Gazpacho," Paolo interrupted.

My parents turned to me then, slack-jawed.

"Gazpacho," I yelled. "It's a cold soup popular in southern Spain—"

"Darling, stop *yelling,*" Mum hissed.

Paolo and Dad waited a beat and then jumped in at the same time—something about his roses. Dad ignored the blunder. His eyes found their anchor just above Paolo's head and he answered his question at such great length it carried us straight through to the end of the meal. But while Dad talked I noticed Mum watching Paolo, taking in his suit, his hair, his every move, from across the table. I noticed a new framed portrait of the president hanging high on the wall above Paolo's head.

While waiting for dessert, I pulled out Paolo's wedding magazines. We each grabbed a few, flipped and pointed, describing what we saw to no one in particular.

"Here's a nice dress!" (Paolo).

"Grey bridesmaids, how awful." (Mum).

"I can't say I understand any of this." (Dad).

Dessert was served—apple pie with ice cream—and Mum started in with the questions again. She wanted to know *why* Paolo had come to a country where he knew no one, and just how *bad* it had felt when his father was taken in the night. "On a scale of one to ten," she asked, "exactly how afraid are you to return, and would you describe that fear as constant or intermittent?" But she didn't wait for his answer. "You say you were seeking refugee status," she continued, "but were you ever actually granted asylum? Were you ever legal to work? Were you a *refugee* or were you an *illegal?*"

Paolo stammered, "Cómo se dice? Cómo se dice?" scanning the floor frantically as if the words he was looking for might be written there. Had his English always been this bad?

When he did manage a sentence, my parents turned to me puffing like goldfish and I had to do an English-to-English translation. Sometimes all three of them spoke at once—questions and answers colliding mid-table. It was the acoustics, I convinced myself. But then I noticed when Mum asked Paolo to pass the cream, their hands both traced blind circles mid-air, unable to connect. And there was that one moment, once the sun had sunk low in the sky, filling the turret with a yolky light, when I looked at him and then, it seemed, through him to his ripe red insides, his hundred snaking veins. It was as if he were a bottled specimen—a tadpole or a skinned lizard—amid all that apricot jam.

I USED TO dream Paolo was made of tissue paper. I'd be running through a wide-open field with him neatly folded in my hand, but then it would start to rain—fat, fierce drops dissolving him. When that tissue paper was so thin it was hardly there, I would rub my palms together, rolling him up until he was pill sized. Then I'd pop him in my mouth and he'd be gone.

In another dream we'd be on the couch talking. I'd lean in to ask him a question and he'd hang his head, searching for the right words. "Answer me," I'd say, an impatient mother screaming in his ear. I'd grab him by the chin and shake him until his face slipped from his head and landed in his lap, like pea soup, or pudding, or face gravy. I'd look up, but there'd just be a blank pad of skin where his face once was. I'd reach into the slop in his lap trying to reassemble his nose, eyes, lips, but I'd only stir things up, making it worse. He would scream if only he could find his mouth.

IN THE FOLLOWING weeks I was the one chasing Paolo from room to room, calling my questions after him: "What exactly were you doing before I met you?" I'd ask. "Who were your friends?" and "What were your plans?" and "Have you been reading my notebooks while I'm at work?"

Every time I entered a room I'd find a stiff wind cutting right through the centre, indicating he'd just fled. Sometimes if I ran fast enough, I'd see his back disappearing around the corner.

I asked and I asked until I got my answers.

Paolo was illegal after all. He'd applied for asylum but, one by one, he'd seen his other Argentine friends get turned down—not enough Credible Fear. Without me, he'd had little hope of getting papers, little hope for the future. Without me he couldn't drive or work or see a doctor or rent a video. Without me he was nobody, nothing, a ghost. He was marooned on the tiny island of the present. But that wasn't the point, he insisted. The point was he loved me. Very much.

His ninety-day fiancé visa expired and Paolo went back to being a refugee. He lost his job at the architecture firm. The only work he could find was the night shift as a security guard downtown. We held opposite hours from Monday to Friday. He started sleeping on the couch. Sometimes I'd peek in, see him curled up with his stacks of bridal magazines and wonder, was I the Supreme Bitch in this situation? I knew what my questions were doing to him: that I was tearing holes in him through which his love leaked out. I saw it happening, but I couldn't stop myself. I was made for this.

Was I wrong to question his motives? Wrong to call off the wedding? Did my discoveries necessarily cancel out our love? Isn't it possible to hold need in one hand, love in the other? Aren't we all refugees when it comes to matters of the heart?

OUR LAST CONVERSATION, if you could call it that, was on a Sunday in February. I'd been chasing him around the house, and had tricked him by switching directions several times. We collided under the tortoise head. I hardly recognized him. He had grown a beard since we'd last seen each other.

"Wait right there," I said. I'd been waiting for this moment for months. I pressed play on the stereo, the tape synched to the right spot. It was Elvis, singing the exact words from Paolo's proposal. I folded my arms, ready to wait out his silence.

Paolo's lips were moving, but only a strangled sound was coming out. He might've been saying "I love you" or "I loved you" or maybe "I loathe you"—I couldn't tell. It was as if something was stealing the words from his mouth, as if he were calling me from another country, using one of those cheap, warbly phone cards.

I looked up at the tortoise head and imagined its body squirming around on the other side of the wall, flippers thrashing to be free of its heavy wooden collar. I looked down at Paolo. The two of them were craning, treading water. The two of them pinched, frozen in time. In some other dimension Paolo was saying all the right things. If only I could hear him.

THOSE LAST MONTHS, I stayed at the office late most nights. I was working on a new side project, Mating Game™—a board game not unlike Trivial Pursuit—except instead of plastic pie pieces, I was thinking of using fake diamonds that fit into a plastic ring. I wanted there to be a box of cards—on one side of those cards, every Question 26 I'd ever written; on the other side, different answers with point values. I wanted all my hard work to come to something. I wanted there to be winners and losers.

When I wasn't working on the design, I was working on my pitch:

Dear Parker Brothers, I have a dream. Bingo, Monopoly, Scrabble: each started with a dream, behind each dream, a dreamer.

Or:

Brothers, It wasn't so long ago courtship began with the handing over of a "confession album," a book of Proustian questions and the answers given at every stage of a young man or woman's life. Isn't it time to bring us back to a more familiar time, to a world where lovers can ask each other, "In what ways do I disappoint you?" and "Who would you be without me?" free of consequence?

Or:

George and Charles, you are brothers but how well do you really know each other? What secrets do you hold in your hearts? Fear not, Mating Game™ is here!

I DON'T THINK I laid eyes on him from March through May, but I could sense him. Most mornings when I woke up, the bathroom walls were still steamy from his shower. I'd enter a room to find a warm spot on the vinyl chair, a book open, a cup of yerba mate and half-eaten toast. I'd hear his soft feet padding in the room next to me. I'd rush forward, calling, "Paolo, do you love me? Do you loathe me?" and "Maybe we can work it out!" but by the time I got there, the room would be empty. I'd find the couch pillows still holding his shape, the smell of him in the room, sometimes more than his smell, the bright dust of him hanging in the air. He was still there, all around me, living off the smallest sliver of the past. Then I destroyed that, too.

While he was at work one night, after polishing off a bottle of red wine, I pushed the TV aside, climbed up on a small ladder and fished my finger into the tortoise's mouth.

What was I hoping to find? Lost words? All the conversations we'd never had? His secrets, black and curled beneath the tongue? I found none of those things, not even the tongue. It had probably been eaten in some South American ritual I would never understand. My fingers brushed up against the prickly stump where the tongue had been and the tears slid sideways across my cheeks. I curled my finger up and punctured the roof of the mouth. It was thinner than I expected, like phyllo pastry. Something like loose tea slid down my arm. Then I reached up into the brain, into the nose. My finger poked around inside the milky eyeball like a worm in a snow globe, then I accidentally punched through the thin skin of the face, scrunching it up in my fist. One second I was tippy-toe on the top of the ladder, and the next I was up to my elbow in turtle.

Soon it was all dust. Something like a turtle-skin collar remained glued to the wood but the rest was airborne. It was in my hair and on my skin. It was in my mouth. His past was everywhere and I was suddenly, devastatingly sober.

IT WAS MUCH LATER when I heard his footsteps in the dark cave of our room. I know it was him because of the smell of garlic and toothpaste. Also because I felt his hands on me, because I had waited so long to feel his hands on me, all over me, because I had memorized his hands. Then his mouth was on my mouth, breathing into me. The time was right. He wasn't saying it but I could feel it. Only love could make him kiss me like that, like he was drinking my face. He was in me and through me to the count of *one, two, three,* and I was just starting to comprehend that love is need and need is love, that you can't have one without some of the other, when he started to come apart in my hands. He was without a past and without a future, caught between worlds, all shivering pixels, his edges thinning out, the molecules of him sloughing off. The most romantic moment of my life. Then I sneezed and he was gone.

THERE'S NO NEED to hide what we do anymore, no need to pretend. Ever since the men upstairs were made redundant and I became boss, I've given my girls free rein. Lord knows they need it. Men these days are trickier than ever, but our techniques have kept pace with the times. Our psycho-emotional profiling is as accurate as the FBI's. Our attachment-pattern analysis and emotional aptitude indicators are all bang-on. And our turnover rate doesn't lie. It seems every weekend one of my girls is getting engaged or holding a rehearsal dinner.

Still, there are times when some good old-fashioned advice is in order. "If it seems too good to be true, that's because it is," I tell my girls, and "Ask yourself, who has the most to gain from this relationship?" Occasionally, if I'm feeling sentimental, I find myself saying, "Better to have loved and lost than never to have loved at all."

Not a day goes by when I don't think I see Paolo. He is huddling with the other refugees outside the Day Labour Office. They are buying rings, making plans, building futures. Other days I feel him. He lands on my lip, a speck, a featherweight. He is a breeze in my hair, a shiver up my back.

He is winter light, the month of December cycling around and around, going out and coming back to me, weakening me every time. Or he comes to me in dreams. I dream of a dragonfly and I love that dragonfly desperately, the way you can only love something in a dream. When I wake up, he is there in the room with me. In the middle of the city, in the middle of the night, right smack-dab in the middle of my life, I have dreamt him and now he has appeared as a small green miracle bumping up against my window, wanting out. I admire his sleek pencil body, in this his insect afterlife. Then I open the window, corral him on three sides and guide him toward it. "Fly, fly away, dragonfly, my love," I call after him. I make going sounds, helicopter sounds—*puh-puh-puh-puh*—to send him off into the night. I am just that big.

REFUGEE LOVE

radio belly

WHO KNOWS WHEN or why a thing begins?

Maybe your childhood bed sat atop the world's most precise magnetic beam, a pinprick shooting off from the earth's core. While you slept, the metals you'd ingested by day tore through your veins to gather in one spot. You dreamt of explosions as blood burst like flares against the dark ocean of your insides.

Or maybe it started before that. Your dad reminds you that sadness lurks at the cellular level, that your mother was sad and her mother and the mother before that. It was always coming for you, unavoidable as runoff. After your mom passed, he used to take you to healers posing as baby-sitters, women who waved crystals above your sternum and criticized your aura—it was too thin, it stopped just below the knees like a torn-off skirt.

It was at one of these women's houses that a tomcat came banging into the house and dropped a hummingbird at your feet. Playing dead with its wings tucked in tight, it was barely thumb-sized. Before you could bend down, the cat swallowed the bird whole, smooth as a vitamin. Then, at some point on the way down, the bird came back to life. In a moment the cat was skittering, crablike across the floor. How that cat howled. How it tossed itself sideways into the furniture, like a puppet with its insides possessed.

Or maybe it starts in your fifteenth year, the first time your body stops belonging to you. You're asleep when your small, souring appendix—Napoleon you will call it—turns septic. You wake to find a deep gouge in your abdomen like you were hooked and dragged around by a drunken pirate.

You cry into your dad's flannel armpit.

"Do you know how lovable you are?" he says and he's crying too, the big sap.

"So brave. I'm so proud of my girl." In the moments when he loves you most he talks this way—about you rather than to you—and you let him. It's just easier.

"Someday someone will worship you and scars won't even matter. Do you know that?" You are still his girl—studious, good, translucent.

You nod and breathe him in—man sweat, mustard, sawdust—but you don't believe a word. Somewhere down in the meat of you there is the slightest murmur, like an argument heard through thick walls.

YOU ARE SIXTEEN by the time the million rebel particles have rearranged themselves into this, the hard, wallet-sized shape pushing up beneath Napoleon's scar. You wake to the distinct crackle of transmission and some other language—Russian? Portuguese?—singing up your spine. *Grikzee-grikzee-grak* it goes—guttural but with pouncing *R*s. Greek maybe?

You aren't worried. Stranger things have happened. That burrowing wart on your heel. Once, an allergy that made your lips swell up like water wings. Another time, a flea trampolining on your eardrum. There've been pinworms, nosebleeds, whole extra teeth nobody warned you about. And your dad's friend with the tumour that was actually her twin. The body as bully, as boss—you get that already.

So that morning you don't tell. You skip breakfast and catch the early bus to school. Right away you feel different. For the first time ever, you take one of the sideways seats at the back of the bus, where all the cool, moody kids sit. The spillover from their headphones sounds like dropped cutlery. Then in biology you ask the loud, hot boy to be your partner. And later, in a third-period group presentation, you blurt something about Stalin's moustache to cover up your *zizz*ing abdomen and make the whole class laugh.

At the end of the day, you stand before the mirror in the pale green light of the third-floor washroom and make up your mind. This noise is the best thing that's ever happened to you. You feel seen for the first time.

You stop off at the mall on the way home from school and blow all your babysitting money. You buy clicky shoes—the kind with the hard plastic soles. You buy fat wooden bracelets that clunk up and down your wrists. You buy huge, gong-shaped earrings and another pair, shaped like tiny mallets. You will wear these things all at once and walk—*click, clunk, gong*—down the school halls.

Lying in bed at night you decide the women in your family weren't sad but misunderstood. Like you, their insides sizzled. Those stories about your grandma who, after a bottle of red wine, would stand up in the middle of a dinner party and sing "Stormy Weather" or "God Bless the Child" out of time and tune, stomping and swaying before her captive audience—maybe she wasn't singing so much as trying to cover up the noise. It could be her voice humming up through your bones now. You imagine all the women of your family crowded into a tiny room of the afterworld—pale ghosts huddled around a transmitter, sending dispatches from beyond.

A ROUND OF layoffs, and your dad is one of the lucky ones. He is switched to nights—asleep when you wake up and gone by the time you get home from school. You leave big cakey muffins on the counter for him with notes tucked underneath: *Passed biology* and *Miss you too.*

By now it sounds like talk radio—all those bright-big personalities, the noise of too much opinion, only in a language you don't understand.

There are times, while conjugating verbs or staring down *X*s and *Y*s in a quiet classroom, when your belly yelps. Times when your abdomen resembles the angry guy on the bus—spitting mad. These outbursts only ever happen at school of course. People swivel, looking for the source. Señorita Estarr's eyes change shape. *Lo siento,* those eyes say. You clutch your stomach, screech your desk across the floor, feigning cramps, kidney stones, chemical spills.

By the time you learn to clench down on all that noise, it's too late. Your name has been added to a list.

Now your free periods must be spent with a woman who makes everyone call her Gert. Gert wears socks with skirts and clothes that look like old curtains. Her hair is mostly fuzz, but the picture on her desk indicates she wasn't always this way. She was someone once.

Gert has a theory: Everything is something else. Anger is really disappointment and disappointment is really grief and grief is really loneliness. She says feelings are ladders, that each step down brings you closer to the source.

"So what's at the bottom?" you ask.

"Of the ladder?"

"Yeah."

That stops her for a moment. A drifty smile floats across her face. Then she becomes very serious and says, "Peace."

YOU DIP INTO your college savings. Your dad keeps the bankcard and PIN in his top drawer under the box of condoms—the one place he thought you'd never look. You buy all kinds of belts—wide leather ones, thick fabric ones that you wrap around your bickering abdomen. The retail girls at the mall see you coming and wink to each other across the bright aisles—*here comes one.* They know your type.

You buy a belly-dancing scarf with little brass bells that jangle. Then, because every girl needs a gimmick, you decide to change your name to Belle. You sew little bells to the hems of your pants, onto cuffs and the ends of shoelaces.

You experience a sudden, violent surge in popularity. It has nothing to do with you, everything to do with the other stuff. You have friends now—hordes of girls with high-tight ponytails. You all dye your hair the same shade of brown and apply tanning lotion to make your skin match. You all cover over freckles and other distinguishing marks with foundation and head to the mall, faces matte as Band-Aids. You shoplift and take rides from boys who think you're a band of sisters. You end up lying under playground slides, drinking Southern Comfort straight from the bottle. The boys paw your clothing, press wet-cold noses to your skin. "It's a pacemaker," you say. "It's a tracking device" or "It's an artificial organ." But they don't care. They are discovering you and seeing past you all at once.

Insatiable, Mr. Holmes writes on the chalkboard: "A kind of hunger that can't be satisfied." When he says the word he licks his lips and quivers, not unlike a teenage boy.

In astronomy you're learning about black holes, event horizons, points of no return. Every time Mr. Karger says "collapsed star" his gaze lands on your left shoulder.

Dissection day, and the first time you cut into flesh it squeaks. Your insides squeak back. You pocket the small dry organs and arrange them on the shelf in your room, hoping they might transmit.

Gert says feelings are onions. Feelings are oranges. Feelings are elevators.

It grows louder. Even your friends think you're whispering behind their backs. Even Gert says, "Is that your phone buzzing?"

It's necessary to develop a new loud personality, one that everyone will like, but this keeps you so busy planning what to say next, you can't hear anyone else. "Are you even listening to me?" your friends ask. Gert is on to you too. Sometimes, at random, she'll say, "Can you repeat back what I just said?" She calls this new trick "Keeping the Mind on a Leash."

It's necessary to develop a new high-pitched laugh. Your laugh goes forth and steals other, smaller laughs. *Infectious,* adults call it, but you know the truth. Your laugh is not a giver. It takes and takes.

You buy perfume that smells exactly like chemical pears. It stings your eyes and makes the back of your throat tingle, but it keeps people away. This perfume is your roar.

Some Sunday afternoons when you're home together, your dad tiptoes as if there were a giant or a baby sleeping nearby. Or a giant baby. You've noticed he doesn't ask for hugs anymore, that his love has a little bit of fear mixed in.

Late at night you can hear the women of your family gathered in that small room. They are agitated now, singing on top of one another. They want you to know you're being stalked by something. It's black and panting and the worst kind of loyal.

You learn to sleep with the TV on channel 100—nothing but static turned up all the way.

IT GETS LOUDER, vibrating from your belly up your throat. It rattles your teeth like teacups on a train.

You want to go out but the noise won't let you. Messages zip up the spine to arrive fully formed in the brain and you don't stand a chance. The command is given—*Stop! Sit! Cry!*—not in words but in blips and blaps, in some secret mother tongue, and your body obeys every time. You are the cat that swallowed the hummingbird.

You graduate, just barely, and all your friends head off to college. You can't face any more quiet classrooms though, so you stay behind. You start serving at the noisiest pub you can find. Friday nights and Football Sundays, the noisier the better.

Your dad, back on days, has girlfriends now—women who hang around the house smoking cigarettes in his oversized shirts, planning your future. *You could work on a cruise ship!* they say. *You could be a model or a dealer at the casino!* and then they discourage you from drinking coffee, soda, booze.

"What's that *noise?*" your dad says when he's alone with you. He looks under the table, inside the cupboards, behind the fridge. "You hear that? Something grinding?"

You slink from the room.

EVERY SOCIAL ENCOUNTER is a threat, something to avoid or smother. You ask short, sharp questions and surround yourself with girls who love to talk about themselves, girls who are always performing for someone on the other side of the room.

Somehow you meet a boy, Jocko. He's in a band, drives a van with no seatbelts and isn't afraid of perfume. He has mastered self-deprecation, a tricky kind of vanity. He has a controlled aloofness, as if he's always measuring himself out in small doses. Best of all, he's preoccupied, trapped inside a bubble of his own private noise. He conquers you with compliments and soon you're moving in together. It might be love.

RADIO BELLY

WHENEVER YOUR DAD invites you for dinner, he wants to know how you're doing, whether you're *really* happy and, if by chance you're troubled, what he can do to help. He wants to know when you'll go back to school, whether you have a "life plan."

When you answer, he winces like the bottoms of his feet are sunburnt. His love has a bit of pain mixed in. His hair has a bit of grey. The shadow of another, better you darkens the air. This other you—who he wants you to be—is in school, reads books for fun and rides her bike everywhere. She's dating someone wholesome, maybe a poet, someone allergic to perfume. On a good day you can feel her—who you could be—screaming inside a glass jar, dangling down the deep well of yourself. If only she could get out.

Your dad's judgment is a type of love—you understand that—but still you attack. You blame him for all the years he worked nights, all the ways he wasn't there, twisting guilt into him like a screw. You wish he understood this is also a type of love, an acknowledgment of history. But you take it too far every time. This is how you begin to hate yourself.

You finish eating in silence. The distance between you crackles.

LIVING WITH JOCKO is great right up until he discovers he's not the centre of your universe. Then it's like holding your breath. At any moment he might discover what's really at your centre—a corridor of noise, an industrial static. Fear, your four-legged friend, follows you around the house, licking your hands, the backs of your knees. You want to confess or to escape or to say *Let's try again later,* but you're afraid if you open your mouth now, your teeth will shatter—teacups turned to dust.

YOU FINALLY DECIDE to see someone, one Dr. Palmer at a clinic near work. He was Irish once and talks like he has a mouth full of marbles.

He moves the cold metal stethoscope around your belly. His hands are pudgy, "Peach" from the Crayola box and too young for the rest of him. He tilts his head this way, then that, listening.

"So?" you say.

"So," he says, straightening up, "it's a racket in there." But he's not surprised, too old for that.

He says he'll put you on a list for a specialist and then asks if you're old enough to remember Lou Sealball. This Lou person once picked up spy transmissions through her fillings, he says. Driving through the desert one night and next thing she knew, Japanese spies chattering away inside her molars.

"So this has happened before?" you ask.

"My dear," he says, pulling out the necessary forms, "everything has happened before."

At home you Google Lou Sealball and get something to do with the Macy's parade. It will be years before you figure out he meant Lucille Ball.

YOU SEE ONE very expensive Dr. Sitwell.

"Do you like yourself much?" he asks.

"Do I what?" *Lick-lick* goes Fear—rough-tongued, meat-smelling.

"That's what I thought," he says, folding his hands in his lap. "I sense some unhelpful self-talk. In just six to eight sessions I could raise your self-love from a zero to a seven."

He assigns homework—"Sensory Deprivation for Self-Discovery." You are to spend hours by yourself, transcribing all your inner self-talk and then bring it back to him for evaluation.

You go home. You sit. You listen and write.

"Lumping around," Jocko calls it, although he scratches at the door from time to time. He has ditched the band and gone solo. He's experimenting with sensitivity and a new shaggy hairstyle. He's made it his mission to cheer you up. His whole new personality depends upon it.

"Sensory deprivation," you explain, although you think of it as something else: receiving, deep-sea diving, noise mapping. "It's a therapy thing. I'm not *supposed* to be happy."

But Jocko is relentless. "We should get new furniture!" he says. There are couch deliveries, new dishes, something called nesting tables, something else called a multichannel amplifier. There is cardboard and newsprint. There is bubble wrap. Then everything is in its place again and there is a deadly quiet, a long life of comfort stretching out ahead.

"IT'S ALL VAGUELY Japanese sounding," Dr. Sitwell says, looking over your homework—pages and pages of mangled words. Then he assigns new homework—to attend church services in other languages. It's the best practice for Compassionate Comprehension he says, which is the first step toward Decoding of the Self.

You visit Greek Orthodox, Portuguese and Haitian churches in far-flung neighbourhoods. You sneak in late and take a pew near the back. Still, people hear you coming. They glare or move away.

Then one day you find a Russian Church, the last beautiful thing in a rundown part of town. The inside is basic, with bare concrete showing in places, but that only makes the stained glass more impressive. It's as if those other churches have the wrong idea, as if, after a point, beauty cancels itself out.

A woman is kneeling up ahead. Her elbows are hooked on the pew in front of her and she's making thick, phlegmy promises to God. You open your jacket and, for the first time, give your noise completely to the room, sending it up like prayer.

When you open your eyes again the woman is standing over you, Compassionate Comprehension written all over her face. She slips onto the bench beside you. She pets your hair, pulls your head to her shoulder. She is clucking for you, crying for you, like your long-lost Russian mother.

"WE SHOULD get a dog!" Jocko says, and just like that there is a black puppy, Hex, bumbling through the apartment. There is whimpering and walking—endless walking—and pee on the living room floor.

You spend your days trying to make outside noises match your inside noise, which means listening to the same songs over and over again—sad girls with guitars, angry girls with guitars. Then you try to match the way you feel inside and outside. You begin to peel your fingers. Tweezers and a kitchen knife. The sting. For a moment you achieve the perfect balance, pain for pain.

"I'm almost done decoding myself," you tell Jocko. "It won't be much longer now."

But Jocko gets tired of his new personality, and yours. He patches things up with the band and moves out, taking everything but the dog. You lie on the floor wondering if you ever really knew Jocko, if you've ever really known anyone. Hex licks your face, your ears, your hands. He hasn't been fed in days. He sleeps curled up on your radio belly, twitching in dog dreams. He barks at the noise, digs with his paws, licks and licks. Soon your skin will be bruised, then raw, then thin as tissue. Soon Hex will eat you alive.

YOU QUIT DR. SITWELL, and in the alleys of Chinatown find a Chinese Medicine doctor. You duck in through the unmarked door and sit beneath a giant yin-yang tapestry in the empty office. Incense wafts. A fountain burbles. The walls are lined with bottles of shiny black pellets.

When a small white man shuffles out to greet you, introducing himself as Dr. Wally in a thick Chinese accent, you stand to leave. You catch yourself though, stopping to reason: he *is* three times your age and three times your age *should* be old enough to make anyone as Chinese as they want.

Week after week, Dr. Wally asks, "How you feeling?" and then pins you down with needles. He leaves you in a back room for an hour, two, while your insides calm from a roar to gentle womb sounds. He prescribes all kinds of black pellets and puts you on a heavy-metal cleanse. You imagine your veins scraped clean, glittering dust falling from the vaulted ceilings like fish scales.

Sometimes after an hour of lying on the table, listening to the pot-clanging sounds of Wonton Alley, needles in every limb, there is an upswell of something like whale music, wolf music—half whimper, half howl.

You tell Dr. Wally about the music.

"Chi rising," he says. "You no worry about that."

Every time you leave Dr. Wally's you feel quieted down. You try to maintain the feeling, moving through your day as if balancing a cup of green tea on your head, but it never lasts. You aren't Chinese enough.

"Forget the needles," you say to Dr. Wally one day. "I need you to just go in there with your hands and find some knobs. Just reach in there and change the channel."

"We cannot change body," he says. "We can only meet body halfway. We must learn to speak Body." He shuffles into a back room and returns with a twig to boil.

YOU WERE PERFECTLY sterile about it. No shower curtain— Jocko took that. No Hex—you could hear him on the other side of the door. You lay on a perfectly clean sheet in the bathtub and cut fast with an x-acto knife. The pain was nothing. Then you opened the wound—that hurt a little— and dug your fingers in, hoping for metal, an oyster's pearl, something foreign. You remember a hard shape, but it was sensitive, inextricable and all grown over by veins. It was part of you. There was something like a nipple where you'd hoped a knob would be, something fleshy-hard like the tip of a nose, and all the blood. After that you don't remember a thing. And now here you are, in the hospital with a friendly figure floating toward you as if on roller skates—your dad.

"Why didn't you tell me you were so sad?" he asks. He doesn't wait for an answer. "That's okay. I found my girl just in time." He covers your entire forehead with kisses.

In the days that follow he sits by your side hoping to talk, but you're distracted. All you can think is how tired you are. This is the tiredness that broke the camel's back. The tiredness that killed the cat. That jumped over the moon.

The women of your family are lulling you, making ocean sounds now—*shhhh, shhhh, shhhh.* It isn't silence you've achieved exactly—it's deeper than that. It's the clean, clear whoosh of white noise. It's static or something like it.

floatables:
a history

AFTER THIRTY-ODD YEARS of living on the land I built
with my own hands, I am once again adrift in a
drowned world. Every day the seas recede, giving back new
land, but I won't be fooled. From the safety of this crooked
old boat I see the jungle vines hanging like nooses. I hear the
thrum of flesh-eating insects. And more than once I've seen
cannibals scurrying in the underbrush. The earth is healing,
scientists say. Mother Nature is giving us a second chance,
but the Mother Nature I know is a she-devil all dressed up
in green. It's just a matter of time before she rears up, ugly as
ever, to show us all who's boss.

I'm one of the oldest, old enough to remember the flood,
and the time before that too. I remember solid land and
twinkling cities, nothing but the music and lights and perfume of civilization as far as the eye could see. I remember a
person could live in such comfort at the top of such tall tow-
ers, they could go days without touching ground. Then when

they did, they wore the most impractical shoes, just because they liked the look of them—shoes with heels, shoes with wheels, shoes with lights. I remember what any six-year-old would: grocery stores stocked to the roof with ketchup and SpaghettiOs, birthday parties, pony rides and my big pink bed. But all that decadence couldn't last.

Mother Nature turned on us. Earthquakes, hurricanes, mudslides, tsunamis: you name it, she dealt it. Then she melted our icecaps. The seas rose up and our glorious cities were gulped down, all our lovelies and our valuables too. Art and music, jet planes, calculators, schools, hospitals, malls: all went into the drink. And what got burped up? What bobbed to the surface as evidence of all that human progress? Plastic and rubber, canned goods, little packages of soya sauce and relish, flip-flops, stir sticks, Styrofoam cups, diapers and coffee lids. Such a vast and disorganized carpet of garbage that I've spent half my life trying to make sense of the civilization it represents.

Luckily, Daddy had a plan. We spent our last days on land stocking a little rubber boat with everything we would need. "It's into the human soup or die, Twyla," he announced before we pushed off our rooftop for good. And he was right. What land remained was so crowded, so rife with human competition, it made the people vicious, wild. I won't tell you how bad it got except to say that the lucky ones drowned.

For months it was just me, Daddy and his briefcase in our rubber dinghy. Sometimes we would come across jagged green peaks of land, and I would plead to be taken ashore, but Daddy wouldn't allow it. "We're sticking to the plan, dollface," he'd say and he'd look out over the horizon, waiting for I didn't know what.

Eventually we arrived at a place in the middle of the ocean where the water went around and around, a place thick with bottles. "Recognize it?" Daddy asked and I did, from TV and from all those *National Geographic* posters he'd plastered around the house. It was the Great Pacific Garbage Patch, "bellybutton of the world," as he liked to call it.

He put me to work right away. I spent days fishing for plastic bottles and matching caps, screwing them up and then tossing them into a big net he'd rigged up behind us. Once our nets were full, once we had so many bottles it looked like we were towing mountains, we started tying them together with seaweed by moonlight. It was on these long, watery nights that I first turned to the moon for comfort—another kind of dinghy floating in another kind of sea. It was so full and bright in those days, maybe because we were that much closer to it or maybe because the rest of the world was so vast and dark.

"What are we doing, Daddy?" I sometimes dared to ask while I lashed bottles into floating bricks.

"Building a continent, sweetpea," he would answer, looking harried.

I'd seen Daddy this way before. Those days, back on land, when he'd pick me up from school, pulling me down below the city, on and off trains then back up into the university library where he'd spend hours at a long wooden table, walled in by stacks of books. He'd explained his work to me once or twice. He was developing a new breed of rubber tree, a hardier version that wouldn't need tapping. Instead of soil, its roots would survive on plastic, he said, because of a built-in micro-something that would devulcan-something else. If only I'd paid more attention. What I did know is the roots of Daddy's tree would exude white milk that would turn to rubber, something his bosses at DuPont were very excited about.

From the safety of our dinghy, we lashed all those bottles together, building upwards and outwards until we'd created a huge floating pyramid with a wide skirt of shore. Then Daddy climbed up, cracked open his briefcase and pulled out a hearty sapling. He shook it free of the goop that had kept it alive those months at sea and coaxed its roots around a plastic Coca-Cola bottle.

Daddy's plan was sound. His rubber tree took to the Coke bottle and the next bottle and the bottle after that, binding them all together until, not six months later, we had a peaked and beautiful island with our tree standing at the top, its roots sunk deep into the thick, white, rubbery ground. The land went so far upwards we had shade at certain times of day, so far outwards we could walk ten minutes in any direction. "As far as the eye can see," Daddy said, and if you stood at the bottom of the hill and squinted, he was right.

It turned out we had made land just in time too because the sea was suddenly full of babies and toddlers, humanity's last great hope, set adrift. Every day they appeared on the horizon on rubber rafts, in dinghies and bowls, pushed by currents toward the ocean's great navel. Daddy trolled as far and wide as he could, returning home every day with a new brood, becoming Daddy to all. He turned away every last swimmer, though. He was obsessed with all things mouldable by then and didn't want anyone over a certain age. Except for Peggy O'Hare. When she paddled up to him, a pregnant teenager, so large and helpless, he bent all the rules.

For over thirty years we rose up out of the sea like a fine white bone. In all those years, not a broken arm, not a bruise or stubbed toe because rubber can be just so kind. When the weather got bad, we pushed off to warmer climes. When the sea rose up, we bobbed: indestructible, bouncy, floatable.

But this is the beginning of the beginning. You'll want to know how Mother Nature caught up to us, and why it is we are at sea once again. For that, I'll have to start at the beginning of the end.

FIRST CAME THE smoke—three huge, twisty columns rising up where sea met sky as if the seam of the world were on fire. We huddled on the shores of our island, leaning into the breeze that had leaned on us for thirty-odd years, and watched the wind whip that smoke into secret alphabets spelling our future, that and animal shapes, too.

"Look, a honeybee! A swan!" the little ones screeched, carrying on the way children do: pretending to be familiar with things they've only ever heard stories about, even as the snot runs down their faces.

Peggy thought it was her son Vern on his way back with a boatload of the same crap he'd started hauling ashore once the rubber ran thin: coconut bras and conch shells, wood and weavery, animal heads and hides—things from the natural world that would've been banned in Daddy's day. I didn't see how Vern could possibly have anything to do with that smoke, but Peggy moved from one cluster of islanders to another, spreading her rumours regardless.

At the sight of smoke on the horizon, even Tex, the second-oldest islander, had come down the hill to hand out grim wisdom. He knew as well as I did that smoke could only mean trouble. "That there's an omen," I heard him say, pointing out to sea. "Not the good kind either," he went on, but that part was lost to the wind like so much that matters.

Tex had shown up sometime after Peggy all those years ago—a pimply teenager paddling a tin bathtub. By then Daddy had grown soft. When he wasn't out fishing for pickles or canned peaches for Peggy, he was by her side, rubbing her feet. So Tex had been allowed to stay. For three decades Tex had been up on the hill writing the history of our island—"The Book" he called it—and building a crooked old boat in the shadow of my museum. The boat was something like a patchwork ark, although he didn't call it that. He called it the "Damn Thing" and was always going on about how it would one day save us all.

Like Peggy, I worked my way down the beach that day, but with a different agenda.

As the town historian, and Daddy's only true daughter, it was up to me to remind people that even though our rubber tree had started to wilt, even though the seas were low on canned goods and we'd eaten nothing but refried beans for months, we must still stand by Daddy's plan.

"You know we used to float past other islands from time to time?" I started with the first young man I saw. "You know how green and jungly and wild they were? How filled with cannibals? And the women with bare breasts slung together as hammocks for their young? And the men with leaves over their dangly bits and an appetite for little boys' ears?" Here I reached up and pinched the young man on the ear, just to make sure he was listening.

"Course, Granddaddy knew those islands would drown and they did. That's why he made all this," I continued, laying a hand on the young man's shoulder, guiding him away from Peggy and the others. "Every last one of those islands was gulped down without so much as a hiccup." A silence here while I let him imagine it, then a well-timed question: "You think it's a coincidence it's only us with the rubber, and only us that survived?"

The young man stiffened when he realized we'd reached the end of the beach and I was starting him up the hill toward my museum. "Now, you might be thinking our old rubber tree's dried up," I said, tightening my grip on his shoulder. "You might be thinking it's time for us to abandon rubber and 'go green,' but I'm here to tell you, I've found a new rubber source floating out at sea—if only I could find someone brave enough to go get it." Here I pressed a scrap of black rubber tire into his hand. "Now it may be black," I said, "but it's rubber all the same." Before he twisted away I was able to look him in the eyes and say, "Black is the new white!" Then I headed back down the beach to try and wrangle another young mind.

AFTER THE SMOKE came the barges: one steely grey and one the colour of rust, both with tall sides and big windows that bounced the light. Those barges rose up over the curve of the earth, then sat about a mile off shore, buzzing and clicking like jungle insects. Twenty-eight days they stayed out there, cranes and drills up to God knows what. I remember Daddy talking about barges of roaming scientists, men of knowledge who had saved themselves from the flood, and all I could think was maybe they'd know a thing or two about rubber with the built-in devulcan-what-nots and where to get more, maybe they'd have something to eat other than beans—maybe ketchup! Maybe SpaghettiOs!

Peggy and her friends were stationed two-by-two the whole length of the beach by this point, scanning the horizon left-right, left-right all day like a bunch of scrappy seabirds. They were even sleeping down there, acting as though it was just a strategy to get first pick of the goods when Vern arrived. But I knew something bigger was going on. I heard their whispering. The last time so many had camped out was when islands had started to reappear on the horizon. These same women had thought it their place to monitor the situation then. They'd developed all sorts of superstitions, believing they could induce an island's reappearance with ritual and prayer. From up on the hill, I'd hear their whooping and hollering whenever the horizon rearranged itself. I'd see their strange animal dancing, and once or twice I thought I smelled smoke. That's back when I urged Vern to borrow my boat and set off in search of distant rubber—white rubber, I was clear on that. While Peggy and her friends had been dancing on the beach, I'd been poring over Daddy's old papers and I'd come up with a great equation.

Did he think it was a coincidence, I asked Vern, how much our island resembled the moon? Wasn't the moon the only other land we knew that was as permanent and as dry, the only other piece of untouched real estate? What we needed was some fresh white rubber, I said. Then, to spur him to action, I reached into my own secret stash and gave him a taste from what might very well have been the last bottle of ketchup on earth. It had the desired effect. He moaned and closed his eyes for a long time, and when he finally returned from those flavourful throes, some crucial part of him belonged to me.

He'd come back every few months with a bright-coloured catch of Tupperware, rubber duckies and balls, saying that's all there was out there, asking for another taste of the "good stuff." I'd give him a taste but I would always refuse his rainbow of rubber, sending him right back out saying, "Try harder" and "Go farther." My first mistake: believing a patchwork island was the worst that could happen. Every time he returned he'd bring along boatloads of contraband goods—fruits and feathers, fur and bananas. One time he came back with the new name Vern, although he was born Steve. Another time he came back with a pretty little wife. And then, finally, he returned with an idea. He came up the hill to see me straight away.

"What about black tires?" he wanted to know. He said the sea was full of them, that they were an inexhaustible resource. "Besides," he asked, "isn't the moon mottled dark and light? Can't black be the new white?" Something was alive and at a gallop in his eyes. It was the same look I'd seen on Daddy's face when we were stranded at sea all those years ago—the look of a man who's about to become a stranger to himself.

I scolded Vern that day and refused him any ketchup—my second mistake. He marched right back down the hill in a huff, and later that night I heard drums beating down by the shore. I saw shadowy figures wheeling around what could only be the orange light of a fire, the air full of the deep, sorrowful smell of burnt rubber. I closed my door tight and tried not to let my heart fall into synch with their rhythms while I dusted the "Footwear and Technology" section of my city exhibit: high heels and Nikes, CDs and cell phones. That was the last I'd heard of Vern until this business with the barges.

FROM DAY ONE through twenty-eight, Peggy's friends camped on shore, watching those barges. Walking amongst them with my bucket and brush, stopping here and there to paint fresh rubber over a green or brown smudge, I couldn't help but notice how their hair was tangled into thick ropes that stuck out every which way. I noticed their dirty feet, overheard their speculation. They thought the ocean was being sucked up into the belly of those boats, that those boats were responsible for the abnormal weather and the ever-receding tides. I even overheard one woman telling the children Vern had sent the boats to save us. She'd been teaching the children about Mother Nature. I could see the pictures she'd scratched into the rubber at her feet: a fish, a tree, a cloud, fat arrows in between—something to do with the life cycle, with systems and returns.

"Shhhht," I interjected, stooping to paint over her work. "Mother Nature's a witch. Can anyone tell me what a tsunami is? How about a hurricane?"

The children scrammed, but I could see something had been stirred up in them. *Who was this Mother Nature really?* they were wondering. *Why had she forgotten our island?*

THE MEN WHO finally rowed to shore were so different from us and from one another, it was as if they'd been burped up whole from the continental past. But they stuck together, moving as one, like the digits of a single hand. As town historian, I was persuaded to make notes. *Three different colours,* I wrote, *pinkish, yellowish and brown.* I was pleased to see they were older than me, hopeful that they were wiser. Then they opened their mouths.

"We're men of science," said the pink one.

"With awesome equipment," said the yellow one.

"Yeah, check it out," said the brown one, holding up some sort of plunger.

It was our language they were speaking, but the words were all wrong, their voices a startling arrangement of highs and lows. *Accents!* I wrote.

The youngest islanders gaped and crowded around, not knowing any better than to trust men of science.

"We're here to take samples," the pink man said.

"Hope that's cool," said the brown one.

"We'll have, like, a town meeting," said the yellow one, "show you what we found."

I let Peggy lead them around that day and I hung back, making notes. These weren't the pale men of science I remembered seeing on TV as a child. These men had scruffy beards and dirt under their fingernails. The yellow one had a nose ring, the pink one shells in his hair, the brown one had inky blue marks all over his skin. I noticed that they weren't interested in our rubber homes, that they seemed offended by my "Ode to the Coke Bottle" exhibit at the centre of town. Every once in a while they would bend down and, with small, sharp scissors, cut into the ground at their feet, but they didn't seem as interested in the rubber they peeled back as in the green fuzz growing beneath it.

We were standing before a wall covered with the crude math of imbeciles—*A.E + B.C 4ever, Sam wuz here,* and *I ♥ Trees* etched into every last surface—when I suddenly saw our island through their eyes; how grey and thin the rubber, how murky our gene pool, what we'd become. I stepped forward then and gave a long speech about the days when we were gleaming white.

"Now that our rubber tree is near dead," I said, wrapping it up, "we've been considering other options. Maybe black tires. The moon is mottled after all—"

I would have kept on, but they interrupted.

When was the last time we had moved in relation to the other islands around us, they wanted to know, and how long had we been "locked into" this "temperate" climate. It was true, the landscape had stopped changing long ago, and the climate was far from ideal, but I didn't want to think about any of that just then. *Fascinated by all the wrong things,* I wrote. Then I added, *Just like the Peggys,* because I'd grown tired of writing out *Peggy and her friends.* I herded the men toward my museum. "You might be interested in my 'Summer in the City' exhibit!" I said. "You haven't by any chance come across a bottle of Heinz ketchup in your travels, have you?"

I REMEMBER the last fresh coat of rubber laid down—the Big Pour, we called it.

People had been demanding more land, and Daddy, always one to please, had delivered. For the first time ever, he'd tapped the tree's trunk to get buckets of milk. He'd gathered more plastic bottles and then made a big ceremony of pouring the rubber over top, even though he knew as well as I did it could have been put to much better use. The rubber on our island had become thin. The outer shores were jiggly and loose, old chewed-up plastic bottles slipping out from under the island's rubber skirt.

After the Big Pour, the tree's milk slowed to a trickle. How I pleaded with that tree. How I sang to it and prayed beneath it.

Luckily, Daddy didn't live long enough to see the rubber crack and peel up in layers, exposing not a world of plastic but a boggy green slime beneath. He didn't have to endure endless weeks of refried beans or face the fact that, indeed, our island seemed to have stopped drifting much farther north than was desirable, that for the first time in thirty years we were experiencing four distinct seasons, low clouds, endless rain.

IN THE LAST few years, I tried to tell Vern I'd changed my mind about the tires, that black really could be the new white, but he had other plans and kept his distance. Tormented as I was by memories of being stranded at sea all those years ago, I was unable to venture out to sea myself. I could only stand by and watch as the jungle vines snaked up the rubber walls of my museum, as the ground became moist and fertile beneath my feet.

I had no choice but to try and recruit the island's youth. No choice but to pillage my own collection of the treasures that had washed ashore over the years. From my "Modern Woman" exhibit I took Lee Press Ons and fake eyelashes to give to the girls. From my "Things with Wheels, Things with Lights" exhibit I pulled toy cars and glow-in-the-dark key chains to give to the boys. Once I had them seated all around me, treasures in hand, I'd start in about the true horrors of the jungle.

"Do you know the word *carnivorous?*" I'd begin.

I'd tell them how, in those long months at sea, Daddy would occasionally have to swim ashore for food or water, leaving me alone on the dinghy in a dark, dark sea. I'd explain how Daddy would return in the early mornings mud-caked, blood-streaked, bruised and scraped and how, the one time I asked him what had happened, he said the jungle was "carnivorous," that it would eat a man alive given half a chance. "You must never, ever go into the green alone," he warned and then he flashed that look—the one that meant he was on the other side of some threshold I could never cross.

Here I'd pause for another one of my well-timed questions: "Now, after all he went through, how do you think Granddaddy would feel seeing you all today with your contraband bananas and coconuts?"

They didn't have an answer to that.

Sometimes I'd let the guilt settle on them, thick and heavy. Other times I'd push it further, telling them I saw trees dripping with meat all those years ago, and people in the underbrush, wild and fearful as monkeys. I'd say I saw the ground spit like a temperamental baby, that occasionally a bubble would rise up from the mud and when it popped it would release the voices and smells of those trapped below, or their still-warm blood, or their half-digested bodies.

Those kids would hear me out, I'll give them that, but then they'd go back down the hill and persist all the same, going wild after Vern's boatloads of goodies. In just a few short years the people had transformed our island. I saw the potted plants in people's kitchens. At night I could hear the groan of rubber, could smell something like the wet, hot mouth of the jungle closing in on me.

AFTER A LONG day of showing the scientists around our island, we all made our way through the rain to the town meeting they'd convened. Some claimed it was uncharacteristic rain. "Isn't it oily?" and "Doesn't it split the light funny?" they asked, hoping to be remembered as the one who predicted trouble, as if it wasn't obvious trouble was already upon us. We crowded into the schoolroom and waited, shuffling, trying to suppress the sounds of our growling stomachs while the men fiddled with their equipment and a cloud formed above our heads. *Bean-smelling fog,* I scribbled, for accuracy's sake.

Just then the pink man stepped forward. With a single movement of his finger, a light came on and a picture appeared on the wall behind him. "This is our state-of-the-art underwater drill," he said. "We used it to pull a sample from the ocean floor." *Pink man: magic finger,* I wrote before being distracted by the brown man.

He was peeling an orange—I recognized it as soon as I saw it. The peel released a fine spray into the hot lights of their machine and then the smell hit us—a sweet spiciness, an unthinkable, drinkable smell—and we swooned. *Brown man: delicious,* I wrote.

The pink man started talking about mineral sedimentation, algae and plankton, but it was difficult to concentrate because the yellow man was now weaving through the audience with little trays of food he'd prepared—pineapple cut into slices, peanuts in the shell. Before I knew it, there was pineapple in my mouth and I had travelled right out of myself.

The pink man was still talking. "… Analysis shows that your landmass has had a change of heart," he said. Behind him a picture of a green island appeared. Music swelled— now strings, now drums, now a tinkling like rain.

Beside me, the yellow man demonstrated how to twist the peanut shell, how to extract the nut. He kept bending into the lights and I was admiring the way they shone through him, making a blood map of his torso, like so many streams snaking toward lower ground. *Yellow man: thin skin.*

The Peggys were moaning, mouths full, pineapple juice dripping down their chins. They were rattling their peanuts to the music like tiny percussion instruments, giggling at Mother Nature's good humour while the pink man continued to mumble, "... Miraculous, the way the vegetation of the ocean floor has fused with the roots of your rubber tree." He rose up onto his toes. "It seems Mother Nature has given you a second chance."

The yellow man was now passing out sprigs of lavender, cinnamon sticks, pink, fragrant flowers. People were *ooh*-ing and *aah*-ing and I was finally starting to understand what was going on here: sensory warfare. But before I could act, the brown man was at my side with a handful of what looked like driftwood shavings. "Ketchup chips?" he asked. Again, I was unable to resist, my will suddenly rubbery.

"Folks, beneath all this rubber, your island has gone green!" the pink man announced at last. He said something about how our island would blow its rubber cap any day now, then, with his magic finger, he conjured one moving picture after another. Of barren ground. Of rain and then sun. Of something poking through. Then a whole sprouting-unfurling-reaching-creeping sequence. Then jungle with fruits and flowers the size of human heads. Then the whole slithering-crawling-stinging-biting insect nation. Then people kissing flowers, kissing animals, kissing babies, as if that had anything to do with anything.

I'll admit I was swept up for a moment. For a moment I had thoughts about the breathable earth, about forgiveness and all the amazing ways the world had gone about healing itself. For a moment I marvelled at Mother Nature, her generosity, the miracle of this second chance. Then, just before the show came to an end, just before the pink man announced, "You'll all need to come aboard the barge for a few days while the island completes its transformation," I saw Vern in one of their pictures: Vern, playing the bongo drums for some bare-chested island-types; Vern, the only other person who knew I could be undone by ketchup chips. So Vern *had* sent these boats. So these *weren't* real scientists trying to persuade us to go green. The potato chip turned to dust in my mouth.

I stepped forward and introduced myself, again, as the town historian and Daddy's only *true* daughter. I asked the men to please cut us free from the ocean floor and then pack up their show and be on their way. We would do just fine without them. We were indestructible, bouncy, floatable, I said. All the rubber and food we would ever need was bobbing out there in the ocean, if only I could find someone to haul it in.

Then all hell broke loose.

The Peggys were in hysterics. Children were grabbing chips and peanuts, shoving them into their mouths. The scientists were going on about *miracles* and *forgiveness* and Tex was quoting from The Book—something even I hadn't read because he had the only copy. He was reading a description of this very scene—three scientists come ashore to poison the minds of the good islanders. This was always the way with Tex. He'd claim to have written these things long before, but in truth he was changing what had already been put down, lining it up with reality right there in the moment. He'd been writing his book for three decades and I guess he figured here was his big chance. So he was reading away about our drowned cities, about long months in a bathtub pushing through a sea of bodies. I would've stopped him except I noticed the scientists were starting to shuffle and twitch. Thing is, Tex is one of those people who'll make you question your ideas about what's crooked and what's not, even on a good day. The way his left side looks to have fallen off the spine, it seems he's always on the verge of capsizing. To see him then, tilting seawards and reading about *the water closing in like the icy hands of God* and *the bodies floating up like bloated rice* would put the fear in anyone.

WE LEFT THAT meeting in all kinds of disharmony—I know because I followed after the different factions, taking notes.

Some went home and set to work organizing their lives into three piles—essential, not-so-essential, and junk—amazed at how easily a life gave itself over to these stark categories. While they packed their boats, they told themselves the story that comforted them the most. It was of a beautiful island that died a natural death and all the smart and wily people who got away. The next day these people said their goodbyes and we were all a little surprised by their lack of feeling as they paddled off to taste a wilder, greener world, the island shrinking to a little grey dot behind them and inside them.

Meanwhile, the Peggys relinquished all their worldly possessions, and spent their last days dancing nude on the beaches, howling and making love until they blistered in tender places. Then they lined up quietly and were ferried in an orderly fashion to the barge offshore. We could see them standing on deck, waving back at us, waiting smugly for the island to complete its change.

Others, who vowed to love the island and stick to it, spent their final days boxing heirlooms, scrubbing floors and wrapping dishes, because life keeps on demanding right up to the end, and because destruction is, after all, beyond logic. At the end of each day, when their work was done, they gathered to remind each other that they had endured a great test of character, that by resisting the temptations of the wider world, they proved they had honour, loyalty and a proper respect for history.

Tex took to the water to practise his front crawl, his duck dive and deadman's float.

I set to work documenting it all. The beginning of the end.

On the dreaded day we awoke to a high-pitched whine rising up from the ground, as if overnight we'd been pinned to the back of something wild. It was the usual end-of-the-world stuff, the same business we'd managed to bob over for three decades. A heavy wind circled, gathering fear atop regret atop guilt with each pass as if we were a human stew at a slow boil. When the ground started to shake and everything creaked and groaned and exhaled a fine yellow dust, we gathered at the foot of the hill for whatever comfort we might offer each other. We complimented ourselves on our decision to stay, said it was the best choice, the right and only choice. We held hands and trembled even as our houses folded like wet cardboard. We only parted once the ground started to rumble, splitting off to take shelter in whatever places we'd chosen in our final days. Some clung flat to the ground. Some cowered against buildings, under desks or beds, each with a different idea about where to be when an island has a change of heart. While the ground bucked and slapped, we closed our eyes and prayed. We stayed that way, eyes pinched tight against the end of everything while the wind howled and whinnied, while the sea gurgled and spat, and while everything we'd ever known to be upright fell down around us.

Eventually, everyone must've emerged from their chosen hiding spots. They must've looked around at the new landscape—all those places where the jungle had burst up through shredded rubber, and congratulated each other on their bravery, their stick-to-itiveness. Imagine that, they must've said, all this time, rubber as a straitjacket on something so wild and resistant. All this time, the jungle growing strong beneath their feet, Mother Nature healing and forgiving. Then they must've set about going wild themselves, painting their faces with mud and putting bones through their noses, because that's what all that green will do to a person.

I SAY MUST'VE because I didn't stick around to see it. As soon as the ground stopped shaking, Tex and I—the only two wise enough to know better—sprinted over the new ups and downs of the land toward the hill. When we finally arrived, we discovered that, in all that shaking, most of my museum had slid down the hill into his boat. And so, without questioning the wisdom behind it, we set out together.

Now here we are, adrift again, this boat so crooked it almost makes Tex come out right again. There've been times on a moonless night when we've had to feel around for each other in the dark, just to know we're not alone. Days, too, when the fog makes it impossible to tell up from down, when you can start to feel swallowed up by so much grey. It brings great comfort to reach out, days like these, and find a warm pair of hands reaching back.

Turns out the math on this boat is surprising: turns out one plus one is three. So now it's us and you—a floatable family in an endless sea.

The sea continues to recede, giving back land, green and raw, but we wait instead for the world above or the world below. In the meantime I've begun to fill the pages of your father's book with some kind of history so you will know where you come from, a stronghold amidst so much that is watery and changeable in this world. Until then the three of us float, rootless, unbound. Until then you are our moon and we look to you for light.

Acknowledgments

A HUGE THANK YOU to my family: Grandma, for setting me on the path; Mom, for holding me together; Dad, for keeping me on the path; Dylan, for knowing me better than I know myself; Alexander, for inspiring me and supporting me when it mattered most; Sue Mac, for always telling me I can; Kaia Scott, for often showing me the way. Thank you Ryan Buckley for always being willing to talk about ideas. Thank you Susan Housel for the sanctuary. Thank you to George and Ruth Nicklas for your generosity in the final stages of finishing this book.

Special thank you to my editor, Barbara Berson, for so much guidance and patience; to Chris Labonte, for believing in me; and to my agent, Hilary McMahon, for always knowing exactly what to say.

A world of thanks to Zsuzsi Gartner for helping me find my voice. Without you this book wouldn't exist. Thank you to the faculty and staff of the UBC Optional Residency MFA program. And endless gratitude to my fellow writers and friends—Zoe Stikeman, Laura Trunkey, Una McDonnell, Jason Brown, Miranda Hill, Lisa Baldiserra, Lori McNulty, Melanie Schnell and Vicky Bell—for your generosity and expertise and for being my constant muse.

BUFFY CRAM'S fiction has appeared in *Prairie Fire, The Bellevue Literary Review* and the bestselling collection *Darwin's Bastards: Astounding Tales from Tomorrow*. She has spent the last decade teaching and writing in Vancouver, Montreal, Boston, Texas, Mexico, South Korea, South America and various parts of Europe. She currently lives in Berlin.